™

RGIRL™

CURSE OF THE ANCIENTS

BY JO WHITTEMORE

My name is Kara Zor-El. When I was a child, my planet, Krypton, was dying. I was sent to Earth to protect my cousin, but my pod got knocked off course, and by the time I got here, my cousin had already grown up and become Superman. I hid who I really was until one day when an accident forced me to reveal myself to the world.

To most people, I'm Kara Danvers, a reporter at CatCo Worldwide Media. But in secret, I work with my adoptive sister, Alex, for the Department of Extra-Normal Operations to protect my city from alien life and anyone else that means to cause it harm. I am . . . Supergirl!

The Library of Congress has cataloged the hardcover edition as follows:
Library of Congress Cataloging-in-Publication Data
Names: Whittemore, Jo, 1977- author.
Title: Curse of the ancients / by Jo Whittemore.
Other titles: Supergirl (Television program)
Description: New York : Amulet Books, 2018. | Series: Supergirl ; 2
Identifiers: LCCN 2017057405 | ISBN 9781419728662 (hardcover POB)
Subjects: | BISAC: JUVENILE FICTION / Action & Adventure / General. |
JUVENILE FICTION / Media Tie-In.
Classification: LCC PZ7.W617828 Cut 2018 | DDC [Fic]--dc23

Paperback ISBN 978-1-4197-3610-0

ABBO40383

Cover illustration by César Moreno
Book design by Chad W. Beckerman

Published in paperback in 2019 by Amulet Books, an imprint of ABRAMS. Originally published in hardcover by Amulet Books in 2018. All rights reserved. No portion of this book may be reproduced, stored in a retrieval system, or transmitted in any form or by any means, mechanical, electronic, photocopying, recording, or otherwise, without written permission from the publisher.

Printed and bound in U.S.A.
10 9 8 7 6 5 4 3 2 1

Amulet Books are available at special discounts when purchased in quantity for premiums and promotions as well as fundraising or educational use.
Special editions can also be created to specification. For details, contact specialsales@abramsbooks.com or the address below.

Amulet Books® is a registered trademark of Harry N. Abrams, Inc.

ABRAMS The Art of Books
195 Broadway, New York, NY 10007
abramsbooks.com

PREVIOUSLY IN
™

National City has seen its share of trouble. But weeks ago, a rare Atlantean metal, orichalcum, was released into the air after an explosion. Regular citizens began to exhibit superpowers with enough force to rival National City's own hero—Supergirl. She and her friends at CatCo and the DEO had their work cut out for them. The orichalcum gave these supercitizens enough power to wage an epic battle. But thanks to Supergirl's quick thinking, and a little superpower that too often goes unnoticed—logic—the supercitizens were defeated. The orichalcum was returned to Atlantis, along with its guardian. And National City returned to its normal, quiet pace, with only one superhero at the ready when she's needed.

Things have been quiet in National City ever since.

But there is always quiet before the chaos . . .

1

THE RUSTLE OF PAPER.

A soft cough.

And then . . . a violin's bow hummed across the A string.

Kara Danvers smiled as the sweet note pierced the near silence. A second later, the note grew into a melody that made emotion swell in her chest. If Kara's eyes hadn't been closed, everyone in Noonan's restaurant would have seen them fill with tears.

Just as swiftly as the music brought her down, it lifted Kara once more, and her smile returned, her cheeks forcing the tears to spill over.

The music stopped.

Kara opened her eyes.

"Miss Danvers, are you all right?" Hannah Nesmith, the curly-haired woman seated across from Kara reached out a hand.

"Oh, gosh, yes!" Kara laughed and removed the headphones she was wearing. "I'm so sorry. That was just . . . amazing." She removed her glasses, as well, and wiped her eyes with a napkin.

Hannah Nesmith was one of the few (too few, in Kara's opinion) famous female composers in the country. And Kara, who worked as a reporter for CatCo Worldwide Media, had been lucky enough to score an interview with her and hear one of her latest compositions.

Hannah smiled. "I'm glad you enjoyed it."

Kara passed the headphones and music player back to Hannah. "Seriously. I have never had a song *move* me like that!"

Hannah pointed at Kara. "You should hear it with a full orchestra."

"Oh, I don't think there'd be enough napkins," Kara said with a chuckle. "And bravo, by the way, for your skill on the violin." She clapped, and Hannah blushed.

"I actually play the flute in this piece; the person you just heard was Claude." As she said the name, Hannah's blush deepened.

Kara pursed her lips. "A good friend?" she asked with the innocence of someone pretending not to pry.

Hannah smirked at her. "You could say that. We play for the same orchestra, but we met during a triathlon."

Kara's jaw dropped. "Hold up! You're a ridiculously talented composer, musician, *and* triathlete?" She leaned toward Hannah and whispered, "Are *you* Supergirl?"

Hannah shrugged and laughed. "Maybe. She and I are never in the same place at the same time."

Kara laughed, too. *If only you knew you were sitting right across the table from her,* she thought.

Kara probed Hannah about her triathlon hobby, which had, in turn, led to Hannah's inventing an app for note-taking on the go. Kara flipped through the notes *she'd* just taken on a steno pad, shaking her head.

"Hannah, I would seriously kill for a fraction of your talent," she said.

"Oh, please. You and I aren't so different," Hannah said. "We're both writers who speak to people through our work."

Kara snorted. "Yeah, but *my* work doesn't sell out shows at National City Music Hall."

"But it could sell out a TED Talk," Hannah replied. "By this time next year, you could be in Vancouver, giving a speech on women in media."

Kara smiled. "I don't see myself ever going to Vancouver."

Their server arrived with the bill, and Kara plucked the check holder away before Hannah could reach it.

"Dinner is on CatCo," she said, even though she was pretty sure her boss, Snapper, would scoff at the idea. She'd once seen him drink from a coffee cup labeled ~~NO MORE~~ NEVER MR. NICE GUY.

Kara extended a hand to Hannah, who shook it. "This was such an honor, Ms. Nesmith. Thank you for meeting me so late in the day."

"Anytime," said Hannah. She leaned toward Kara. "And even though the performances are sold out, I've got VIP passes, so if you want to come with someone special . . ."

Kara smiled. Her someone special was Mon-El of Daxam, but his home world had been a party planet, where people were unlikely to listen to classical music. Anything without inappropriate lyrics was probably not going to be on his radar. Still, Mon-El had been spending a lot of time at National City Museum learning about ancient civilizations. Maybe Kara could convince him to expand his interests to classical music as well.

"I'd love to go," Kara told Hannah. "Thank you."

"I'll leave two tickets at Will Call," Hannah said. She glanced at her watch and grimaced. "I hate to eat and run, but I've got another appointment."

"Yes, go, go!" Kara waved her away and placed some money in the check holder.

Hannah smiled gratefully and rose from her chair,

colliding with a tall, sleek-haired brunette. Kara perked up when she realized it was one of her best friends, Lena Luthor.

"Oh! I'm terribly sorry. Are you all right?" Lena reached for Hannah's arm, and her eyes widened. "Hannah Nesmith! What are you doing here, of all places?"

"I just finished an interview with *CatCo* magazine," said Hannah, gesturing to Kara. "This is—"

Lena's face brightened. "Kara!" She opened her arms, and Kara stood and stepped into them, smiling.

"Hey, you! What are *you* doing here?"

They separated, and Lena nodded to a nearby table of suit-clad men and women. "I'm at a business dinner as well." In a lower voice, she added, "I'm hoping they'll fund a cancer cure I'm developing."

Hannah Nesmith laughed and shook her head. "Leave it to you to find a cure for cancer, Lena." She turned to Kara. "You want to talk talent? Back in school, Lena was a fencing master, a Chess Federation champ, *and* she finished two MIT Mystery Hunts in under twenty-four hours." She elbowed Lena. "But you left the coins for other people to find. So sweet."

Lena ducked her head. "You speak too kindly of me, Hannah." She squeezed her hands. "Are you in town for a bit?"

Hannah nodded. "I'm at the Wayward Arms if you want to catch up."

"I'd love that!" Lena's eyes flitted back to her table. "And now, I really must dash."

"Go get 'em!" Kara cheered.

Lena winked and hurried off.

"I'm afraid I have to go, too," Hannah told Kara. "If you have any more questions, please feel free to call." With a wave, she departed.

Kara watched both women walk away, visionaries and dynamos of the twenty-first century. Back when Kara had been Cat Grant's coffee-fetching assistant, Lena and Hannah had already been wowing the world with their talents.

The thought made Kara feel a bit . . . unimpressive.

Yes, she was Supergirl, but only because of Earth's yellow sun. And as Kara Danvers, she'd finally moved on from being an office assistant, but she was a barely recognized reporter.

Meanwhile, Hannah Nesmith was running triathlons, inventing apps, and composing symphonies, while Lena Luthor was mastering anything she even glanced at.

Neither Supergirl nor Kara Danvers could compare. But maybe she could change that.

Under the cover of darkness, Kara slipped into the alley behind Noonan's and leaped into the night sky. She soared over rows of buildings before touching down on the balcony of DEO headquarters.

The Department of Extra-Normal Operations was like her second home *and* office. Here, she worked for a Green Martian named J'onn J'onzz who posed as the human DEO director Hank Henshaw. His second-in-command was Kara's sister, Alex. But as Kara glanced around the control room, she didn't see either of them. She did, however, spot another one of her best friends, Winn Schott. He was sitting at his desk, a pen held between his upper lip and nose like a mustache while he tufted his dark hair and stared at a laptop screen.

"Hey, Winn?" Kara said as she approached him. "Have you seen J'onn or Alex?"

Winn let his pen fall into one hand and swiveled to face her. "Yeah, they're on the roof."

"The roof?"

"You know." Winn pointed up. "Big square thing above us that keeps the rain out."

Kara pinched his arm. "I know what a roof is, smartie. *Why* are they there?"

Winn grinned and squirmed out of her reach. "Apparently, there's a big comet coming. Dr. Hoshi brought her telescope, so everyone else is going to check it out."

Kara raised an eyebrow. "But you're not? Isn't this what you live for?"

When he wasn't inventing or hacking something, Winn was absorbed in science fiction and obsessed with outer space.

Winn scoffed. "Please. I've been to another planet *and* have the space rocks to prove it." He polished his fingernails on his shirt. "Once you've crossed the galaxy, everything else pales in comparison."

Kara smirked. "You're saying this to a girl who's crossed *several* galaxies."

Winn stared at her. "Let me have my moment, Kara."

She laughed. "Fine. But I still find it hard to believe you aren't interested in seeing the comet."

Winn shrugged. "It's orbiting Earth for five days, so I'll have plenty of chances to see it."

Kara crossed her arms.

He smiled sheepishly and pointed to his bag. "I may have a portable telescope I plan to break out later."

She nodded. "There we go. What are you working on now?" Kara started to turn his laptop in her direction, but Winn reached out and steadied it.

"Hey, hey, hey!" he said. "I'm doing some personal shopping."

Winn's cheeks turned pink.

"Are you buying more action figures, Winn?" Kara asked teasingly.

He shot her a look. "First of all, they're *collectibles.*

Second"—he turned his laptop so Kara could see the screen—"I'm buying a gift for Lyra."

Lyra, an alien refugee from Starhaven, was Winn's girlfriend. She was a bit of a wild child, but she had a good heart.

"Awww!" Kara squeezed Winn's shoulder and glanced at the screen. "That's ador . . . mat." She frowned. "That's a doormat, Winn."

He grinned at her. "Yeah, but look what it says." He enlarged the image, and Kara read.

"There's no place like 34.1546° N, 118.3340° W." Kara shook her head. "I don't get it."

"It's the latitude and longitude for my apartment!" Winn tapped his chest. "I'm giving Lyra a doormat for my home because I want it to be her home, too."

Kara gasped. "You're asking her to move in with you?" She squealed and bent to hug Winn. "That's great! And a *really* clever gift idea."

Winn leaned back in his chair and smiled smugly. "Just call me Mr. Terrific."

"Heh. Now I know a Mr. Terrific on *two* Earths." Kara glanced at the screen again. "Wait a minute. Winn? That doormat is a custom order." She clicked on a link. "And they aren't sure when it can be available."

Winn blinked at Kara. "Well, yeah. I didn't say I was ready for Lyra to move in *now*."

Kara rolled her eyes.

"Oh, don't judge me with your judging judgery." Winn waved a finger at Kara. "Lyra's out of town, and I miss her, so I'm keeping busy." He closed his laptop and slid it into his messenger bag. "That's why I'm about to meet James for patrol. You're welcome to join us."

"James" was James Olsen, one of her closest friends. He'd been sent to National City by Kara's cousin, Clark Kent, to watch over Kara before she became Supergirl. He now ran CatCo during the day and fought crime at night under the guise of Guardian, with Winn monitoring from a surveillance van.

"Thanks, but I need to talk to J'onn," Kara said, pointing up.

"If you change your mind, we'll be out all night." Winn stood and slung his bag over one shoulder. "You can find us at the corner of Danger and Excitement."

Winn walked away, whistling "Space Oddity," and Kara grinned. Then she zoomed out the balcony doors and up to the roof. Several uniformed DEO agents and one in a lab coat were gathered around a telescope; J'onn stood off to one side with Mon-El, Alex, and Alex's girlfriend, Maggie Sawyer.

At Kara's sudden appearance, the foursome stopped talking. J'onn, Mon-El, and Alex smiled, while Maggie stamped her foot and groaned.

"Aw, man!"

Alex held a hand out to her girlfriend, palm up. "That'll be five dollars."

Kara narrowed her eyes good-naturedly as the money changed hands. "Do I want to know what you were betting on?"

Mon-El raised his hands defensively and greeted Kara with a kiss. "For the record, babe, I didn't participate."

"Neither did I," said J'onn.

"We saw you flying toward the building," Alex explained to Kara. "Which, by the way, you should *not* be doing in your street clothes."

"I'd bet Alex that after you found out where we were, you wouldn't have any interest in joining us," said Maggie. "Because you've seen enough of space for a lifetime."

Maggie was one of the few people outside the DEO who knew that Kara was also Supergirl. The fact that Maggie worked for the National City police and had never revealed the secret made her an ally in Kara's book.

"And *I'd* bet that my little sister, who has the most curious mind in the universe, wouldn't miss seeing this comet for anything." Alex put an arm around Kara's shoulders. "And I was right."

Kara gave her sister an apologetic look. "Actually, I came to talk to J'onn."

Alex dropped her arm from Kara's shoulders, and Maggie let out a "Ha!" before snatching her five dollars back.

J'onn stepped closer to Kara. "You wanted to talk to me? What about?"

With Alex, Maggie, and Mon-El all listening, Kara blushed and adjusted her glasses.

"I was hoping I could start doing more for the DEO," she said quietly.

Mon-El smiled. "Doing more than protecting this city every day?"

Kara shook her head. "Not as Supergirl. As Kara Danvers."

"What?" Alex's forehead wrinkled in confusion, but Kara pressed on.

"I'm already familiar with a lot of alien species, but maybe I could specialize in something," Kara told J'onn. "Like alien weaponry. It would be good to know what I might face."

Plus, it's definitely something Lena Luthor and Hannah Nesmith won't be experts at, she thought.

J'onn stroked his chin. "We've got some artifacts in the subbasement you could look at, I suppose."

"That's a start," Kara said with a nod.

Alex nudged her. "Why are you going into DEOverdrive? Is everything OK at CatCo?"

"Of course." Kara gave her a reassuring smile. "I just want to . . . expand my interests."

And be a little more impressive without my cape, she added to herself.

"OK," said Alex, though she still looked puzzled.

"We can head downstairs after the comet appears," J'onn told Kara. He checked his watch. "Which should be any moment now."

J'onn beckoned for Mon-El, Maggie, and the Danvers sisters to follow him to the telescope, where the woman in the lab coat, Dr. Hoshi, was telling the other agents about the stars overhead at that moment. Normally, she acted as the DEO's physician. But tonight, the petite Japanese woman stood on tiptoe to point out a constellation.

"Want me to lift you a little higher?" Kara asked with a smile.

"Kara! Glad you could join us," Dr. Hoshi said in greeting. "And no, thank you. I prefer to keep my feet on the ground." She glanced down at the rooftop. "Or the concrete, in this case."

Kara gestured at the telescope. "I had no idea you were into astronomy."

"It's kind of my secret passion," Dr. Hoshi confessed. "Tonight, we're going to observe Caesar's Comet. Have you heard of it?"

"It was *not* named after the salad," Mon-El chimed in. "And if you suggest that, people will laugh." He cleared his throat. "A lot."

Kara held back a smile and rubbed his arm sympathetically. "I'm not familiar with the comet, Dr. Hoshi."

"It was last seen more than two thousand years ago, shortly after the death of Julius Caesar," the physician said. "Many Romans thought it was the deification of Caesar: proof that he'd become a god."

Dr. Hoshi turned to the rest of the group before she made her next comment. "It's also a daylight comet, which means it's bright enough to see during the day, but since it comes into orbit tonight, I thought it would be fun to witness its arrival."

She bent over the telescope and made a few adjustments before turning to her laptop.

"This is it!" Dr. Hoshi announced.

Everyone chattered excitedly and shuffled closer to the telescope.

"I'll adjust the telescope as the comet moves, but please don't linger too long, so everyone gets a chance to see it," she said. "While you're waiting, you should be able to see the comet with the naked eye right . . . there."

Kara glanced to where Dr. Hoshi was pointing and saw an ice-blue dot against the star-speckled darkness.

"Too cool," Alex whispered beside her.

Kara turned to answer but was blinded by a brilliant flash of light. All around her, people cried out in surprise.

The whole world had gone white.

Mon-El gripped one of Kara's hands, and she felt around for her sister with the other.

"Alex!" she cried.

"Kara!" Alex called.

Just as she touched her sister's fingers, a wave of energy slammed into Kara, knocking her hand loose from Mon-El's.

She felt herself falling.

Then everyone and everything went silent.

Before Kara hit the concrete, the white light faded to black, and she passed out.

2

KARA OPENED HER EYES TO A sunlit room where she was lying on the world's most uncomfortable couch.

Though she could feel a flimsy cushion beneath her, she could also feel a hard platform beneath *that*. And the pillow under her head had all the softness of a folded paper towel.

Kara lifted a hand to rub her eyes and froze. Before she'd passed out, she'd been wearing a pink sweater and black slacks over her Supergirl costume. Now she was looking at a familiar blue sleeve with a thumb-hole cuff.

"Ohhh, someone knows I'm Supergirl!"

She scrambled to a sitting position, her red skirt and cape fanning around her as she hunted for her sweater and slacks. But all she saw was a crude-looking sack dress folded neatly on a wooden stool. "And they took my clothes!"

Supergirl felt a twinge of pain in the crook of her right arm. She peeled back her sleeve and saw a tiny puncture mark.

"And my blood! How'd they get my blood?"

Thanks to Earth's yellow sun, her skin was typically impervious to harm.

"With a kryptonite-tipped needle. And don't worry; we only took what was necessary."

A male voice spoke from a shadowed corridor beyond the doorway, echoing across the room . . . a room that was a perfect cube of marble from floor to walls to ceiling, save for a skylight above the couch.

Supergirl had heard the voice before, but she couldn't quite identify the regal tone.

"Who's there? Show yourself, so I can take *your* blood!" she demanded.

The man chuckled, and she heard the clap of leather soles on marble as he approached.

Supergirl leaped from the couch and poised herself to tackle whatever Big Bad was coming, but when the man walked into view, she froze.

"You?" she gasped. "*You* did this to me?"

Supergirl took in the man's blond hair, normally shaggy

but now cropped close and decorated with a laurel wreath. She gaped at his ensemble: a purple tunic beneath a white toga, and below that, lace-up sandals.

"Marcus Gaius," Supergirl whispered.

"I'll bet now you regret tipping me all those times at Noonan's," he said with a chuckle.

Not long ago, Marcus had worked at the restaurant, taking coffee orders. He'd also helped protect National City when the Atlantean metal, orichalcum, had given citizens—including himself—superpowers. During that time, Supergirl had gained an extra power, too, one that hadn't fully left her system yet. She could understand almost any language and even understand the true meaning behind people's words.

Unfortunately, she couldn't understand why a barista like Marcus Gaius was suddenly into kidnapping and blood theft.

"What's going on, Marcus?" she asked.

"It's actually *Gaius* Marcus. I switched my first and last names to fit in here." He held up a finger. "You know what? Call me whatever you wish. We *are* friends, after all." Marcus grinned.

Supergirl narrowed her eyes. "You removed the clothes that were covering my costume. That's not friendly; that's creepy."

Marcus held up his hands. "Gads, no. I wouldn't be so crude. One of my female servants did that so she could draw your blood."

"Oh, that's much better." Supergirl held out a hand. "My civilian clothes. Now."

Marcus smirked. "They're right there." He approached the stool and picked up the sack dress. "See? Pretty." Marcus tossed it to her, but she made no effort to catch it. "I'm guessing you didn't play sports in school," he said, staring at the fallen garment.

"No, and I'm not participating in whatever weird meltdown you're having." She gestured at his toga.

Marcus struck a pose. "This old thing? It's back in style, thanks to you. So's your dress." He held up a finger. "Although it's technically called a stola."

Supergirl frowned. "Back in style? What are you talking about?"

Marcus curled a finger to beckon Supergirl toward him. "Come, come. We're finished here, anyway."

Supergirl didn't move. "What did you do, Marcus?"

"I made National City a bit more . . . livable for some of us," he said, walking away.

As much as she hated taking the bait, Supergirl followed him down a corridor lit with oil lamps until they stopped in front of a pair of wooden doors.

Marcus reached for one of the door handles and winked at Supergirl.

"Prepare to have your boots knocked off."

He pulled the door open, and sunlight filled the corridor, along with an uproarious commotion from outside.

People in togas and stolas were running up and down a dirt-covered street, crying and shouting in confusion as they dodged horses and chariots.

Supergirl's eyes widened, and she whirled to face Marcus. "You've sent me back to Ancient Rome?"

He clucked his tongue and rested a hand on her shoulder. "You don't recognize your own National City, love?"

Supergirl spun back around and studied the scene again.

Across the street stood a building, its door thrown open and a sign painted on the wall beside it in Latin.

FLAPPIN' JACKS, Supergirl read, tapping into her orichalcum-based power.

That was the name of her and Alex's favorite brunch place.

And whenever they finished eating at Flappin' Jacks, they always walked next door to Frosty's for . . .

Supergirl glanced at the next building. It had a picture of a snowball covered in orange syrup painted on its closed door.

Supergirl stumbled back from the doorway. "No," she whispered.

"Yes!" said Marcus. "I had to, you see, for my wife, Valeria. She'd only feel at home here." He closed the door.

"Feel at home? If she wants ancient, why National City? It's full of skyscrapers," said Supergirl.

"Is it?" Marcus grinned, and Supergirl's stomach turned. She dashed back to the skylight and peered out.

There wasn't a single skyscraper in sight.

The city's buildings still stood, but they'd all been reduced to only five or six stories tall.

"Wha . . . how . . . ?" Supergirl pointed at the skylight. "The buildings! Hundreds of people are on each floor!"

"Mmm, yes. They're all alive, unfortunately." Marcus strolled over to join her. "I wanted *authentic* structures from Ancient Rome, but that would've meant collapsing the existing buildings with people still inside." He made a face. "Too much blood in the streets."

"Then how . . ."

"An elaborate illusion," said Marcus. "Outside, the buildings look small; inside, they're full-sized."

Supergirl blinked and landed in front of him. "So all of this is an illusion?"

Marcus laughed. "Oh my, no. Everything else is as ancient as it gets. It's been two thousand years since my

Valeria was up and about. Modern technology would overwhelm her."

"Two thousand years?" Supergirl leaned against a wall, feeling dizzy. "Your wife is two thousand years old?"

"She's not the only one." Marcus bowed low. "As I said, I am Gaius Marcus, son of Lucius Marcus and Flavia Lucretia. And a *curule aedile* to boot." He winked at Supergirl. "Means I'm in charge of big buildings, love."

"*You're* from Ancient Rome?" Supergirl shook her head. "That's impossible."

"Says the flying girl who can shoot lasers from her eyes." Marcus shrugged. "What can I say? I made a deal with the right demons."

"Demons aren't—" Supergirl stopped herself and rubbed her forehead. "A demon kept you alive this long *and* turned National City into a replica of Ancient Rome?"

Marcus held up two fingers. "Two demons. Beelzebub preserved my soul *and* brought my dear Valeria back, while Tempus Fugit changed the scenery."

Supergirl clenched her jaw and stepped closer to Marcus. "What did you give Tempus Fugit in exchange for this version of National City?"

Marcus chuckled and poked Supergirl's shoulder. "You, of course!"

Supergirl grabbed the front of Marcus's toga and tried to lift him into the air, but Marcus placed his hands over hers and pushed down. The force of the thrust reminded Supergirl of the effort it had once taken her to stop a runaway bullet train.

"You are a feisty one," Marcus said with a grin.

"How are you so strong?" she grunted. "I saw you lose your power!"

When the citizens had developed superpowers, Winn had invented a device to monitor their power levels. By the end of a massive superbattle, Marcus had been completely drained.

"I already possessed great strength, thanks to Beelz," Marcus informed her. "What you saw me lose was a power granted by the orichalcum: invisibility."

"Invisibility?" Supergirl repeated, the hairs on the back of her neck rising.

"Yes. And that—sadly, temporary—power came in handy when I needed to plant a few hidden cameras and get a sample of your blood to call Tempus." Marcus's lips twitched in a smile. "Do you remember the night J'onn and Alex gathered the good supercitizens before the superbattle? They found me near DEO headquarters."

Supergirl's jaw slackened. "You were at the DEO?"

"It was much easier to infiltrate than the place I stole

the Kryptonite from," Marcus continued. "You should speak with Alex about increasing security."

Supergirl redoubled her grip on Marcus's toga and slammed him against a wall. "You snake! We trusted you! We—"

Marcus thrust out a hand and squeezed Supergirl's throat until she needed air more than words.

"Please calm down," he said. "You're spoiling my good time." Marcus relaxed his grip, and Supergirl doubled over, coughing.

"If you stole my blood back then," she said between gasps for air, "why did you need more now?"

"I needed your blood and spirit to summon Tempus as Caesar's Comet arrived. But binding the curse that transformed the city requires a daily blood offering for as long as the comet is in orbit." Marcus smoothed out the wrinkles Supergirl had left in his toga. "So I needed a five-day supply."

Supergirl straightened to her full height. "After five days, everything returns to normal?"

Marcus threw back his head and laughed.

That meant no.

"After five days, love, National City will remain like this *forever*." He made a face. "Well, most of National City. The curse's power could only reach so far."

Supergirl roared and charged at Marcus, but with the flick of one hand, he swatted her down the corridor. She landed hard on the mosaic floor, sending up a spray of porcelain tiles.

"Save your energy for protecting my city," Marcus scolded her. "You've seen the chaos out there."

Supergirl glanced up at him in disbelief. "*Your* city?"

"Well, mine and Valeria's." He glanced past Supergirl and smiled. "Speak of the angel . . . how did your bloodletting go, my love?"

Supergirl craned her neck to glimpse the curly-haired woman approaching, and instantly she scrambled to her feet, skittering across the broken tiles.

Valeria was none other than Hannah Nesmith!

Supergirl ran toward the composer, who wore a stola and laurel wreath of her own. "Hannah! It's me, Kar . . . Supergirl," she corrected.

"Hello, Supergirl." Hannah smiled warmly at her. "Any friend of my husband's is a friend of mine."

Supergirl gripped the woman's shoulders. "Listen to me. You are Hannah Nesmith, a renowned composer. Marcus isn't your husband."

Hannah giggled and looked at Marcus. "She is quite a comedian!"

"One of her lesser-known superpowers." Marcus winked

at Hannah before whispering to Supergirl, "Hannah can't come out right now. Valeria's in charge."

"You're . . . you're using Hannah Nesmith's body to hold your wife's soul?" Supergirl sputtered.

"She's the mirror image of my Valeria," Marcus said admiringly. "Plus, I can't use my *wife's* body. She's just a pile of bones." Marcus shuddered. "Honestly, don't be so macabre, Supergirl."

Supergirl clenched her fists. "Get rid of her, or I'll—"

Marcus crossed his arms and snorted. "What? Kill me? I'm immortal."

Hannah continued to smile indulgently at both of them. "Marcus, is it time to go home?"

"It is indeed, my love." He reached for Hannah's hand. "Supergirl, I'd invite you to join us for lunch, but, well, you're no fun." He nodded at Supergirl's sour expression. "Plus, you have thousands of confused citizens out there who could use a comforting word or two."

"Oh, I'll give them a word or two," Supergirl said. "And then they'll turn against you." She smirked. "This city won't be yours for long."

"Ah, but that's the beauty of the curse. The longer they're under its influence, the more Roman the people become. Memories of Disneyland will become memories of the Circus Maximus. Every action, every *thought* will change."

Marcus nudged Hannah away from the front door. "Let's sneak out the back and let Supergirl have her moment." He paused and glanced at Supergirl. "Oh, I forgot to mention that when Caesar's Comet leaves, Tempus will take your life with it, so . . . make amends, fight a lion . . . whatever you'd find comforting in your last days." He smiled and nodded before strolling away with Hannah, whistling softly.

Supergirl remained rooted to the spot where she stood, processing everything she'd learned and seen in the last few minutes. It would do her no good to chase after Marcus. She needed to use what little time she had to reverse the curse.

Her only hope was that the DEO was still standing.

Supergirl marched toward the front door and pulled it open. Steeling herself, she stepped outside and was met with grateful and panic-stricken shouts.

"It's Supergirl! We're saved!"

"Supergirl, what do we do?"

"Help us, please!"

People pressed in around Supergirl and began to trample one another to reach her.

"Please! Everyone, calm down!" Supergirl leaped into the air so everyone could see her. "We appear to be under a curse. I don't know yet how to reverse it, but I'm going to figure it out." She smiled reassuringly at all the upturned faces. "I promise you."

"What do we do until then?" someone asked.

"Try to live your lives as normally as you can," Supergirl said.

"But I drive a cab, and now my cab eats hay!" A man pointed to a horse he'd tethered to a bench.

"And I'm supposed to be on a conference call with Tokyo, but there are no phones!" a woman spoke up.

"And all the buildings shrank!" a nervous-looking woman cried.

Supergirl raised her voice to be heard above the panic. "The insides of the buildings haven't changed, and for everything else, we'll adapt! You're all stronger and more resilient than you think." She pressed her hands together. "I'm begging you to make this work for now. I need time to fix this."

And I don't have a lot of it, she thought.

Slowly, the crowd grumbled their agreement and went back to their business. They might be annoyed, but at least they weren't panicking, which Supergirl considered a small victory.

"Now to see how bad the damage is," she murmured to herself.

Supergirl launched herself higher into the sky, scanning the city as she ascended. All the buildings appeared to be constructed of stone, and the windows were covered with wooden shutters instead of panes of glass. Fewer people than usual were in Pineda Park, probably because the children's play area had been taken over by statues, and the paddleboats were now wooden rafts that barely floated.

Not surprisingly, the football stadium had become a coliseum, the area around City Hall resembled a forum, and the government buildings were now pillared monoliths around a crowded courtyard. Using her super-vision, Supergirl spotted the toga-clad mayor speaking to the people from atop a stone bench.

Supergirl spun in a slow circle in midair. Everything was ancient as far as her eyes could see.

But Marcus had said not *all* of National City had been transformed.

Supergirl took off toward the National City Police Department. Before she reached it, however, she smashed into an invisible barrier. She tumbled several dozen feet before she recovered and approached the same point, more cautiously this time.

Taking a deep breath, she exhaled an icy wind that settled on the inner surface of the invisible barrier like frost on glass. Supergirl touched the barrier and followed it from the inside, up and over the buildings. She punched the barrier with all her might but only succeeded in sending a jolt of pain up her arm. She blasted the barrier with her heat vision, but it remained steadfast.

Marcus hadn't just transformed central National City; he'd trapped it in a dome.

Yet the buildings beyond the barrier were just as ancient. Or were they?

Supergirl fixed her X-ray vision on the barrier. The modern portion of National City appeared, its ancient visage just an illusion, like the missing stories of the skyscrapers.

Supergirl flew away from the barrier and back toward DEO headquarters. As soon as it was in sight, she used her X-ray vision to seek out her loved ones.

"Please be there," she mumbled. A moment later she smiled when she saw Alex, J'onn, and Mon-El staring at what had once been a video wall for displaying surveillance footage and the like. Now it held a hand-drawn map and some rudimentary sketches.

As soon as Supergirl landed on the balcony, a DEO agent in a black toga saw her and cheered.

"Director Henshaw! Supergirl's here!" he cried.

J'onn, Mon-El, and Alex sprinted over to her. Alex had gathered the skirts of her black stola to make it easier to run, but J'onn and Mon-El, oddly, were still in their DEO uniforms. They all wore relieved expressions, though tears streamed down Alex's face.

Mon-El wordlessly lifted Supergirl off the floor and squeezed her tight.

"I missed you, too," she mumbled into his shoulder.

The second Mon-El put her down, Alex wrapped Supergirl in a fierce bear hug. "Kara! Thank God. Are you OK?"

"I'm fine." Supergirl blinked back her own tears as J'onn's arms enveloped her and Alex. "Just glad you're all here. Where are Maggie and Dr. Hoshi and the others who were on the roof with us?" she asked, stepping back.

"Maggie's patrolling the city," said Alex. "And Dr. Hoshi's in the infirmary, *on* an exam table for once."

"When the comet struck, she stepped into its path and took most of the blast," added Mon-El.

Supergirl gasped, and Alex held up a hand. "She's OK, she's OK!"

"After being hit by a comet?!" Supergirl squeaked.

"I know, it's weird," said Alex. "But we've been watching her vitals, and they seem fine."

"The other agents who were on the roof are back on

duty," said J'onn. "You were the only one we couldn't account for." He gripped Supergirl's shoulders, checking her over. "You gave us quite a scare."

"Sorry," Supergirl said, sniffling. "My kidnapper should've left a note."

Alex led Supergirl to a chair. "Now that you're safe, tell us who took you. And *why*."

3

ALEX WISHED SHE HAD A GLASS OF water. Or a gallon of it.

Because each sentence of her sister's story deserved a spit take.

"We're under a curse that's turned the center of National City into a version of Ancient Rome," said Supergirl.

Spit take.

"Marcus, the barista and supercitizen who worked at Noonan's, did it."

Spit take.

"With the help of a demon."

Prolonged spit take, followed by coughing.

Alex, J'onn, Mon-El, and the other DEO agents hung

on Supergirl's every word until she'd finished her account of what had happened since the previous night.

It was *much* different from Alex's.

The last thing Alex remembered after the blinding flash was gripping Maggie's hand while they searched for Kara. Alex and the other stargazers had all passed out and woken on the rooftop to find Kara gone, the sun up, and a strange new (or rather *old*) city around them. Stranger still, their rooftop was now only six stories from the ground, but when they went inside the building and looked out the window, they were up as high as usual.

"So Marcus is the evil genius behind all this?" Alex gestured to their antiquated surroundings. "I can't even picture him splashing hot coffee on someone." She paused. "I could picture him *spilling* hot coffee . . ."

Supergirl barely smirked. "Apparently his coy clumsiness was an act to get closer to me *and* to the DEO." She chewed her lip. "Sorry, J'onn."

J'onn placed a hand on Supergirl's shoulder. "None of us saw this coming."

"*I* did," Mon-El grumbled. "I knew Marcus was trouble from the beginning."

"You thought he was a romantic competitor, not a time-turning psychopath," Alex corrected.

When the citizens had developed superpowers, Marcus had been flirting with both Kara *and* Supergirl. Apparently, Mon-El still wasn't over it.

He curled the fingers of his right hand into a fist, knuckles cracking. "Forget Ancient Rome. I'm gonna knock Marcus back to the Stone Ages."

Definitely not over it.

Supergirl put a hand over Mon-El's fist. "*You* aren't going after him at all. That'll just make things worse."

"Hot heads and short tempers aren't what's needed," agreed J'onn. "What's important is finding a way to reverse the curse." He glanced at Alex, who pulled herself up to her full height and smiled encouragingly at Supergirl.

"And we will," said Alex. "Especially with your life on the line."

But Alex projected more confidence than she actually felt. This situation was far different from their typical alien-trying-to-destroy-the-world crisis. At the moment, the DEO didn't have any modern-day resources, and their most useful asset, Winn Schott, was nowhere to be found. From what Supergirl had told them, Alex could only assume that Winn was outside the dome.

Lucky for him.

Alex missed the world of yesterday, when her biggest concerns were getting a reservation at Il Palazzo and justifying to the government the DEO's need for more female field agents.

"What I can't understand is why J'onn, Mon-El, and I are still in our regular clothes while everyone else is in Roman garb," said Supergirl.

"It could be that since we're not of this Earth, the curse didn't affect us," J'onn mused aloud. "You *are* speaking English to Mon-El and me, and Latin to them." He gestured at Alex and the other agents.

"I am?" Supergirl asked, astonished.

At the same time, Alex said, "We're speaking Latin?"

Despite their present predicament, J'onn chuckled. "And I get to enjoy your surprise in both languages. Although to make things easier, maybe we should all stick to Latin."

Mon-El held up a finger. "Uh…I don't know any. Except a few curse words." At a disapproving look from Supergirl, he shrugged. "What? Those are the fun ones."

"If you remain within shouting distance, I can mentally link us so you can understand Latin," J'onn assured Mon-El.

While Alex had no desire to be three hundred years old like J'onn, she envied the Green Martian's skills. Among other things, he could fly, shapeshift, and use telepathy to read minds, *bridge* minds, and fill in language gaps.

"Okay, but stay out of my thoughts," said Mon-El. "That's where I keep my Netflix password."

Supergirl smirked. "At least we've taken care of the language barrier."

"And Marcus did get the DEO colors right." Alex glanced down at her black stola.

"Actually, from what I remember learning at the museum, black was worn by mourners," said Mon-El. He winced at Supergirl. "Based on what you've told us, I think we're mourning your future."

Supergirl sighed and rested her hands on her hips. "Marcus has just the *best* sense of humor."

Alex rubbed her sister's shoulder. "Don't worry. We're gonna fix this."

They turned to watch J'onn, who'd climbed to the top of the stairs.

"Everyone, listen up!" He raised his voice. "Now that we know what—or, rather, who—got us into this situation, we need to find a way out of it. And we have less than five days to do so!"

"Reverse the curse!" Alex chimed in. "That's our mantra. And it starts with tracking down Marcus. If this ritual lasts five days, and he needed Supergirl's and Hannah Nesmith's blood, he's obviously keeping the supply somewhere safe. Let's get his profile up on—" Out of habit, she gestured to where the video wall had been and frowned. "Okay, we're going to need a sketch artist or someone who's really good at Pictionary."

"We also need our sidearms!" Agent Whitby, a man with pockmarked cheeks, spoke up.

"I can manage without my sidearm," said Agent Vasquez, a female agent with short, dark hair. "But I don't even know where to start looking."

"You all heard Supergirl's story," said J'onn. "She was held at a location across from Flappin' Jacks. Our suspect is long gone, but he may have left evidence that could lead us to the ritual site. If you can't find anything in the first location, inquire in the buildings around it. I'm sure any eyewitnesses will be more than happy to cooperate."

Supergirl twisted her hands together while the DEO agents dispersed. "I'm sorry. I should've followed Marcus when I had the chance." She hammered a fist against her forehead. "Ugh! So dumb."

That's a bit harsh, thought Alex.

Mon-El pulled Supergirl's hand down. "Kara, you were in shock. And you did the right thing, getting away from Marcus and coming back to us."

"I guess," Supergirl said with a pained expression. "Maybe Winn can speed up the search." She glanced around. "Where is he, anyway?"

"Winn hasn't come in yet," Alex informed her. "I think he and James were outside the limits of the curse when it struck."

"Oh, thank Rao." Supergirl sighed with relief. "Then Winn's still got his tech. I'm sure he'll come up with something!"

"If there's an impenetrable wall between us, that might not matter," J'onn pointed out. "We need to come up with a solution of our own."

"Agreed," said Alex. She beckoned for Supergirl, J'onn, and Mon-El to follow her to where the video wall had been. In its place was a map of National City that had been inked on parchment. "Can you mark the boundaries of the dome on here?" she asked her sister.

Supergirl raised an eyebrow. "You got a Sharpie under that stola?"

Alex clucked her tongue in exasperation and pointed to Supergirl's eyes. "Use 'em or lose 'em."

"Oh, right!" Supergirl snickered and faced the map. A second later, twin beams of neon-blue light shot from her eyes, searing the parchment and filling the air with the stench of burning, centuries-old goatskin.

Everyone nearby made sounds of disgust and covered their noses.

"Ugh!" Alex coughed. "I slightly regret asking you to do that."

"Why *did* you ask?" Mon-El fanned the air.

Alex peered at the map and tapped a spot labeled PANTHEON within the boundaries Supergirl had marked. "That's why."

The others leaned in.

"A temple?" asked J'onn.

"A demon did all this damage, right?" asked Alex. "Who knows more about getting rid of demons than the church?"

Supergirl grinned and patted her sister on the back. "Ladies and gentlemen, the brains of the family."

Alex laughed and playfully shoved her sister. "I'm sure you would've thought of it, too."

"Nah." Supergirl waved her away. "I don't have a superbrain like yours!" She poked Alex in the side and laughed, but to Alex, the exchange felt . . . off. Especially because as quickly as Supergirl laughed, she stopped.

Alex wrinkled her forehead. "Are you OK?"

"Of course!" Supergirl said in a cheerful voice. "Let's get to that temple."

Mon-El rubbed his hands together. "All right! Let's do this!"

Supergirl bit her lip. "Um…babe? Maybe you should stay here. You can't understand Latin without J'onn, and I can't constantly translate. Plus, I don't want to worry about what you might do if we see Marcus."

Mon-El frowned. "But I'll be on my best behavior. And he can come with us." He pointed at J'onn.

J'onn shook his head. "We have a lot of prisoners here and no technology to monitor their holding cells. I need to assemble a team to keep an eye on them. And, quite frankly, I could use your help."

Mon-El ducked his head and pouted a moment more. "Fine," he finally said, looking at Supergirl and Alex. "But if anything happens—"

"If anything happens," Alex repeated, "we'll call . . ." She cringed and sighed. "Shoot. No tech."

"I can fly back if there's an emergency." Supergirl smiled confidently at Mon-El, and he cradled her face in his hands.

"You be careful, Kara Zor-El," he said.

"As careful as I can be," she promised, and kissed him.

Alex grabbed her sister's hand. "We'll see you in a couple of hours, J'onn."

"Good luck!" J'onn called after them as Supergirl lifted Alex into the air.

"Try not to hit any air pockets." Alex clutched her skirts to her. "The last thing I need is everyone seeing ye olde underwear."

"You know, if Winn were here, he'd point out that 'ye olde' is actually from medieval times," Supergirl said with a chuckle. At a look from Alex, she cleared her throat. "Luckily, he's not."

Alex pointed to the balcony window. "Let's go."

When they were kids, Alex had loved flying with Kara, but now as Alex looked out on National City, she took no joy in the journey. Though she knew the layout of the city like the back of her hand, nothing seemed familiar, and everything looked ancient.

"We're coming in for a landing!" Supergirl shouted into her ear, and Alex clutched her skirts tighter as air billowed upward.

They landed just outside the temple, and Alex's jaw dropped. "I know this place! Maggie's cousin was christened here when this was a Catholic church."

Two men in togas brushed past Alex and Supergirl, headed for the entrance.

"There is a solution, Flamen Dialis, if you would just listen," a man with auburn hair implored his companion.

"You speak nonsense and heresy," said the Flamen Dialis in a dull voice. He wore a round cap, and he had a heavy cloak draped about him. Alex mused that he must be someone of importance. "All things are as they should be."

Alex exchanged a glance with Supergirl. They definitely weren't getting help from *this* guy.

"Please, Flamen Dialis," the auburn-haired man urged.

The Flamen Dialis sighed but nodded. "We shall see

what the augur tells us." He climbed the temple steps, but his companion stopped short. "Well, come along."

"I have someplace else to be," said the auburn-haired man with a slight bow. "But please consult the augur on my behalf." He turned and almost collided with Alex and Supergirl. His gaze flitted over Alex before fixating on her sister.

"That's quite an outfit," he said, dropping the formal tone he'd used with the Flamen Dialis. "You must be something special."

Supergirl arched an eyebrow. "Yeah, I'm a crime-fighting alien."

The man's eyes widened. "You don't say! Maybe we could talk."

Alex sighed and perched on a dusty stone pedestal. Even during a crisis, men found time to flirt with her sister.

"We're kind of busy right now," Supergirl told the man. "And no offense, but"—she nodded at the shock of white running through his auburn hair—"you're old enough to be my father."

The man smiled. "With age comes wisdom."

"We've got plenty of wisdom between us." Alex gestured from herself to her sister.

"Is that why you're sitting on a sacrificial altar?" the man asked. "They used it to burn pig intestines this morning."

In her head, Alex screamed, but outwardly, she smiled and slowly slid off her perch. "I know. I like to live dangerously."

The man raised an amused eyebrow. "Have a pleasant day, ladies," he said, before walking off.

As soon as he was out of earshot, Alex swiped at the back of her stola. "Ugh! Why didn't you tell me this was an altar?" she asked her sister. "Now I'm covered with bacon bits."

Supergirl blinked at her. "I . . . don't sacrifice a lot of pigs, so I didn't know. Could we just . . ." She pointed toward the temple and started climbing the steps.

It took a moment for Alex's eyes to adjust to the dim light inside, but even without the hanging oil lamps and skylight, there was no way she could miss the massive marble figure at the end of the room. The floor at the statue's feet was nearly covered with coins, silver figurines, candles, and jewelry. And where the floor wasn't covered, people knelt with their heads bowed.

Are they actually worshiping . . . whoever this is? Alex wondered.

She was about to say something to her sister, when she overheard a little girl talking to a man beside her.

"I don't like this, Uncle Dan." The little girl clutched his hand. "Everything's different."

"It's a little weird," he agreed. "Do you see your priest anywhere?"

The girl shook her head. "All the people working here are different, too."

Provided by Marcus, no doubt, Alex thought.

"What do we do?" the girl asked her uncle.

"We join the others," he said, picking her up. "And we pray to *our* god."

Alex watched them shuffle to the front of the temple, but her gaze strayed to an elderly man in a hooded toga. He stood off to one side, his hands behind his back, studying the worshipers. Alex tugged at Supergirl's arm and approached him.

"Hi," she said. "We were wondering if you could help us with something." She gestured to Supergirl. "My sister's been cursed, and we'd like to reverse it."

The cowled man frowned. "I can only predict the future. I cannot change the past." He regarded Supergirl. "Have you a liver?" He thrust out his hand, and she stepped back.

"I do. But I'm still using it." She patted her abdomen with a weak laugh.

The man was not amused. "Slay a chicken, and return with its liver. I will reveal your fate then." He tottered away.

"Oh, I already know it," Supergirl said in a small voice.

"Hey, it's going to be OK." Alex took her sister by the

hand. "We'll—OWWW!" Her knuckles crunched against one another as Supergirl squeezed her fingers. "Kara!" Alex wrenched free of her sister's grasp.

"Alex, it's her!" Supergirl whispered loudly.

"Who?" Alex followed her sister's gaze to a woman who'd just approached the shrine. "Who is that?"

"Hannah Nesmith, the woman Marcus is using to host his wife's soul." Supergirl trotted across the room, and Alex followed. "Hannah!"

The woman didn't look up until Supergirl touched her arm.

"Supergirl! What a joy to see you here." Hannah waved to Alex. "I greet you . . ."

"Alex." She extended a hand, but at a confused look from Hannah, she retracted it and imitated Hannah's wave. "Uh . . . Alexandra," she modified.

Hannah smiled. "I greet you, Alexandra. What brings you both to Jupiter's temple?"

Supergirl gripped Hannah's arm. "Hannah, you need to focus."

Hannah glanced at Supergirl's grasping hand in dismay. "I tire of that joke. My name is Valeria Messalina, wife of Gaius Marcus." She tried to shake Supergirl off, but Supergirl's grip stayed strong.

"No, you're Hannah Nesmith, and you like Claude . . ."

Supergirl trailed off and bit her lip. "Uh, just Claude. He's a violinist."

At the mention of Claude's name, the angry V between Hannah's eyes relaxed for a moment but then quickly reappeared.

"I don't know whom you speak of!" she shot back. "Now please leave me alone."

Supergirl opened her mouth to retort, but Alex tugged her arm.

"Come on. You heard the woman." Alex steered her sister toward the entrance.

"Alex!" Supergirl harsh-whispered. "When I mentioned Claude's name, she—"

"I know," Alex said in a low voice. "I saw it, too. And we can use that to our advantage, but not if we make her so mad that she never lets us get close to her again."

Supergirl let out an exasperated groan and rested her head on Alex's shoulder. "I suppose you're right."

"I'm always right. I'm the big sister." She kissed the top of Supergirl's head.

"So what do we do now?"

Alex smiled. "We hide until she comes out, and then we follow her home . . . to Marcus."

They hurried down the temple steps, and someone called to them from a nearby building.

"Ladies! You look a little down on your luck!" A balding, potbellied man beckoned them over. "Perhaps I can help."

The sign above his shop read NO FATE TOO GREAT.

Seeing that he had their attention, he continued his sales pitch.

"I've got amulets, rings, potions, lotions—anything you need to get whatever your heart desires." He smiled broadly and spread his arms wide.

Supergirl glanced at Alex, who shrugged.

"We have time to kill," said Alex. "And he might have something that'll let us reach the outside world."

Supergirl's eyes lit up. "Maybe we can get a message to Winn!"

Heartened at the thought, Alex and Supergirl wandered over to the shop, although secretly Alex knew they wouldn't need anything. There was no doubt in her mind that tech-savvy Winn was hard at work on some new invention and would find a way through to them.

She just hoped he found it soon.

4

WINN SCHOTT BREATHED IN THE salty sea air as he strolled the balcony of his Hawaiian mansion. He reached up to smooth the ends of his awesome, not-at-all-patchy mustache and turned to Elon Musk, who was sitting in a rocking chair.

"By the way, Albert Einstein's joining us for dinner," Winn told Elon. "You're gonna love him, bro. He's the best."

Elon looked up at Winn and was about to say that *Winn* was the best, when Lyra stepped through the balcony doorway.

Winn approached her. "Hey, sweetie! How was the dinosaur safari?"

Lyra smiled coquettishly at him and lifted a hand toward his cheek.

Then she smacked him.

Winn's sunglasses jostled off his face and hit the floor. "Ow! What was that for?"

Lyra scowled at him and spoke in James Olsen's voice. "You need to wake up!"

Elon, Lyra, and the Hawaiian setting around Winn disappeared. He found himself sitting on the floor of a surveillance van, staring up at James.

"Why? What's going on?" Winn rubbed his cheek and then ran his hand across his face, stopping above his mouth. "Awww. No more awesome mustache."

"Winn, focus!" James crouched in front of him, brow furrowed with just a hint of crazy in his eyes. "Something bad's happened."

"Dude, relax." Winn chuckled and patted James's shoulder. "We fell asleep on stakeout. No biggie." He started to sit up, but James grabbed his arm and dragged him to a standing position. "Hey! What's your problem?"

James pushed Winn toward the front of the van and pointed out the windshield. "That. That is my problem."

Directly in front of them was an ancient-looking building, all pillars and angled rooftop. Next to that was another stone behemoth. And another. And another. A few statues of Roman gods were scattered about. And the people strolling in front of the buildings all wore togas.

Winn's eyes widened. "Holy . . . are we in Ancient Rome?" He watched a man herding sheep. "Man, if I'd known this van could time-travel, I wouldn't have haggled over the price."

"We're not in Ancient Rome." James pointed out the side window at a structure beside them.

"National City Bank and Trust." Winn's forehead wrinkled, and then his mouth fell open. "This . . . that . . ." He pointed at the archaic buildings. "That *Ben-Hur* backdrop is National City? What happened to the movie theater and the doughnut shop?"

"I think they're still there," said James. "Just . . . older."

"Oh, man." Winn clambered out of the van and leaped onto the pavement. "How did this happen?" He jogged toward the nearest ancient building.

"Winn, wait!" James shouted after him. "You can't—"

It was like running into a sliding glass door. Face-first.

"Oof!" Winn struck an invisible barrier and fell to the ground. The toga-clad people didn't so much as glance at him. "No, that's OK," he grunted. "I'll reset these broken bones myself."

"I tried to warn you," said James, kneeling beside him. "You OK?"

Winn grimaced and stretched his arms to make sure nothing really *was* broken. "No, James, I'm not. One minute, I'm in Hawaii with Elon Musk and Lyra, and—"

"Love how your girlfriend comes second," said James.

Winn silenced him with a scowl. "The next, I'm trapped outside downtown National City, where almost everyone I know is . . . well, I'm guessing they're trapped inside, since we haven't heard from Kara, Alex, *or* J'onn." He got to his feet. "We should contact the DEO."

"We can't," said James.

"What do you mean?" Winn reached into his pocket, pulling out an earpiece. He slipped it in and tapped it. "Hey, boss. You there?"

No answer.

"J'onn," he tried again. "Alex?" He tapped his comms again. "Hey, Kara, I can't reach J'onn or Alex. Where you at?"

Winn glanced at James, who regarded him with an I-told-you-so expression.

"I've been awake ten minutes longer than you," James said. "Trust me when I say I've tried everything. Watch."

James straightened and pounded on the invisible barrier as a man in a sentry uniform marched past. "Hey! Hey, man!"

The sentry didn't flinch.

Winn got to his feet and tried the same thing, shouting louder than James.

"Hey, buddy! What's with the duck walk?" Winn quickly hid behind James just in case, but the sentry kept marching. "Huh." Winn chewed his lip. "I'm starting to think that that bright light we saw last night wasn't just a blown transformer."

James stared at him. "You think?"

Winn paced in front of the barrier. "So we can't get in, and I'm guessing they can't get out. How far does the barrier go?"

"Let's find out," James suggested.

Winn trotted to the van and climbed in back, James following. Grabbing his laptop, Winn punched a few keys and tried to pull up a live news feed from CatCo Worldwide Media. Nothing but static.

"Looks like CatCo's affected," Winn mumbled, tapping on the keyboard. He went through several more news stations before he found one that was live. It showed aerial footage of ancient National City with a questioning caption beneath: *Dome of Doom?*

As Winn and James watched, a stony silence developed between them.

"Man," James finally said. "It's . . ."

"Everywhere," finished Winn. He reached for his messenger bag. "Get me a map."

"A map?"

"A map of the city. There's one in the glove box." Winn pointed, and James searched.

"It's from 2010," he said, holding it up.

"Doesn't matter," said Winn, uncapping a Sharpie. He took the map from James and opened it on the van floor.

"You're marking the boundaries of the dome," said James as Winn drew. "Why? We can't get in anyway."

Winn leaned back and studied his work. "You'll notice that not all of National City was affected."

James nodded. "Otherwise, we wouldn't be sitting here in jeans and T-shirts."

"Right. So, clearly, whatever did that"—he pointed to the news footage—"had a limit. And I'm assuming it follows the pattern of earthquakes, tornadoes…any natural disaster, really."

James snorted. "This looks like a natural disaster to you?"

Winn held up a hand. "And just like any natural disaster, it has its boundaries and its source. Like the epicenter of an earthquake or the eye of a storm."

"Ohhh." James snapped his fingers. "Which is usually somewhere in the middle."

"Exactly! So if we find the center of this madness, that should lead us to the Big Bad behind it all."

They both leaned forward and studied the map. At the same time, they pointed to . . .

"National City Music Hall," said James. "Really?"

Winn returned to his laptop and clicked through aerial photos of ancient National City until he found one that included the music hall. Now it looked more like a palatial estate with gardens and an atrium. Two red circles with strange symbols inside them had been painted on the roof of the estate.

"What do you think these are?" He pointed to them, and James peered at the screen.

"I'm guessing not helipads," said James.

Winn took screenshots of both circles and folded the map. "Come on. Let's get out of here." He climbed back into the driver's seat of the van, and James buckled up beside him.

"Do you even know where to go?" asked James.

Winn smirked. "My nerd level is over nine thousand, James. I've seen every show and movie involving magic. And the symbols on that roof? Those were magic."

James groaned and leaned back in his seat. "We're going someplace creepy, aren't we?"

"Put on your witch's hat, my friend. We're hitting an occult shop."

•••

Supergirl emerged from the occult shop and frowned at Alex, who was two steps behind her. "Well, that was a waste of time," she said.

They'd been alternating between watching for Hannah and shopping, and neither effort had proven worthwhile.

"Why on earth would I need an amulet to protect me from a drawn sword?" Supergirl wondered aloud.

"Yeah, and a potion to help *me* attract a man?" Alex scoffed. "That shop owner clearly doesn't know his target audience."

Of course, if the shop owner was created by the curse, that makes sense, thought Supergirl.

In a city so huge, Supergirl wondered how many people were real citizens and how many were conjured by Marcus to make Valeria feel at home. And for the ones who *were* real, how long would it be before they adopted the Ancient Roman lifestyle, the way Marcus said they would?

Supergirl sighed. "I hope things are going better at the DE—" She spied Hannah leaving the nearby temple and pointed. "Oh!"

Alex pulled Supergirl behind a statue. "Play it cool. Let's put some distance between her and us before we start tailing." She looked Supergirl over. "And you might want a subtler ensemble."

"Right! Um . . ." Supergirl stopped a man in a hooded cloak. "Hi!"

He pushed back his cowl and gawked at her. "Supergirl!"

"Mind if I borrow that?" She pointed to his cloak.

He blinked in surprise before nodding and handing it over.

Supergirl swung the cloak around her shoulders and raised the hood before turning to her sister. "Shall we?"

Alex motioned in front of her. "Lead the way!"

It wasn't difficult for Supergirl and Alex to stay hidden in the crowd. With no modern technology, most of National City's residents were wandering the streets, looking for something to do. Supergirl and Alex slipped among them like whispers as they followed Hannah.

"She's heading for what used to be the theater district," mumbled Alex.

Supergirl thought back to the map on the DEO wall. "That's near the center of ancient National City. Marcus's curse must have originated there."

Hannah paused to let a chariot pass, and Supergirl and Alex ducked into a shop doorway.

"If Hannah's leading us to Marcus, this is just a reconnaissance mission." It was a statement, not a question, and Supergirl nodded.

"We just want to see where he lives," Supergirl agreed.

Hannah started walking again, but instead of approaching one of the theaters, she turned down an alley.

"Careful." Alex held out a hand to stop Supergirl. "She may be onto us."

Hannah turned another corner and stopped before a building flanked by two enormous statues of . . . Marcus.

Very subtle, thought Supergirl. She turned to roll her eyes at Alex but narrowed them instead as two sentries charged forward with swords raised.

"Looks like someone has bodyguards." Supergirl pointed over Alex's shoulder.

At the same time, Alex pointed behind Supergirl. "Watch out!"

Supergirl spun and ducked just as a sentry slashed his sword where her head had been.

"Really? Beheading?" She flung aside the cloak. "I don't think your boss would be too happy if I died."

The man froze when he realized whom he'd attacked. Supergirl thrust both hands against his chest and sent him flying across the road.

"We might not be allowed to kill *you*," a sentry with a crooked nose told Supergirl. "But we can kill *her*." He sneered at Alex, who balled her right hand into a fist.

"Let me fix that nose." She threw a punch at the sentry, but he blocked it with one hand and swung his sword at her midsection with the other. Alex grabbed his sword arm and pulled him close, kneeing him in the groin.

The sentry doubled over, and Alex stepped to one side, hooking one of his feet and toppling him onto his back.

While they fought, another sentry stabbed at Supergirl with a wood-handled dagger, which she promptly set ablaze with her heat vision. With a shout, the sentry dropped the dagger, and Supergirl head-butted him.

Having felled her previous adversary, Alex wrestled with the fourth sentry, who'd grabbed her from behind. Gripping his forearms, she let herself become deadweight, throwing him off-balance so that he somersaulted forward. Alex knocked him out with a low roundhouse kick to the skull and nodded in satisfaction at Supergirl.

"Who's next?" she asked.

"Me," said a voice from behind them.

Supergirl and Alex faced a barrel-chested sentry who stood several heads taller than they did. His fingertips drummed on the hilts of two sheathed swords.

"Well, this hardly seems fair," said Supergirl. "For you, I mean."

The sentry lunged at her. Supergirl deftly sidestepped him and clucked her tongue.

"You won't even banter with us? That's just bad manners."

Alex cleared her throat and loudly whispered to the sentry, "Also? The swords work better *out* of their scabbards."

A dark smile slowly spread across the man's face. "If you insist."

The sentry unsheathed both swords and slashed at Supergirl's right leg with one of the blades, cutting deeply into her flesh.

But he shouldn't be able to . . .

She couldn't finish the thought.

Supergirl felt as if her leg and her insides were on fire. She staggered and pressed her hands to her chest, feeling her lungs begin to shrivel, her heart to split. As the sentry raised a sword, Supergirl saw a glint of green running the length of the blade.

Kryptonite. Only kryptonite could do this to her.

She dropped to her knees.

"Kara!" Alex ran toward her, but Supergirl shook her head. Marcus wouldn't let Supergirl die before the curse was fully bound, but if Alex didn't keep *her* guard up, *she'd* die.

"What's the matter? Out of breath?" The sentry smirked at Supergirl and thrust one of his swords backward as Alex crept toward him. She bobbed aside, narrowly missing a sword point in her rib cage.

Supergirl wasn't going anywhere, and the sentry knew it, so he swiveled in Alex's direction, wielding his blades in a figure-eight pattern.

"I'm going to enjoy this," said the sentry. "Killing you while your sister watches."

Alex crouched and stepped sideways, foot over foot as she and the sentry circled each other. Supergirl watched her sister's gaze flit from the man's feet to his knees to his ears, targeting weak points.

Quick as a cat, the sentry lunged, swinging one sword high and one sword low. Alex leaped back, and the sentry slashed both swords on a downward diagonal. Supergirl winced, but Alex again dodged with a sidestep.

Supergirl dragged herself toward the fight. If she could just summon the strength to use her heat vision . . .

Alex stomped on one of the sentry's feet and angled a kick to the side of his knee. It made a sickening pop, and the man roared, leaning forward to clutch it. Alex brought her hands to either side of his head and clapped him hard on the ears. He dropped on the spot, and Supergirl called out to Alex.

"Sheath his swords!"

The kryptonite would lose its effect, and a blast from her heat vision would turn the sentry's armor plates into *hot* plates. But either Alex couldn't hear or didn't want to.

Instead, she took one of the sentry's swords and held the point against his throat.

"Tell me how to reverse the curse!" Alex demanded.

The sentry chuckled. "You can't reverse it."

Supergirl tilted her head to one side as her orichalcum-based power let her hear the true meaning of his words.

You can't reverse it alone.

Supergirl sat up a little straighter. So, the curse *could* be reversed.

"And," the sentry added, "you shouldn't have expected a fair fight."

What?

Supergirl scanned the area in front of her. Suddenly, two more sentries leaped out from behind her and ran toward Alex, spears drawn.

"To your right!" Supergirl called.

Alex glanced at her, which gave the pinned sentry a chance to twist his legs around Alex's and flip her onto her back.

"No!" Supergirl shouted.

Before Alex could recover, the sentry clambered to his knees and crossed his swords on either side of her neck.

"Hey!" A woman's voice carried from across the road. "Leave them alone!"

Supergirl shifted to see the woman and gasped.

Dr. Hoshi was running toward them, twirling a bag above her head like a loaded sling.

"Dr. Hoshi, get out of here," Alex said in a strained voice. "And take my sister with you!"

Supergirl tried to wave Dr. Hoshi away, while the sentries watched with amusement.

"No. She should stay." The sentry holding the swords grinned down at Alex. "Then she can take your head back as a warning." The sentry flexed his arms, and Supergirl cried out.

"Alex!"

"STOP!" Dr. Hoshi shouted, thrusting out a hand.

It glowed with the same white light that had struck National City the first night of Caesar's Comet.

The light shot from Dr. Hoshi's palm and blasted the sentry's breastplate, launching him through the air. He crashed into a statue of Marcus and crumpled to the ground, his swords falling from his hands.

Supergirl gawked at Dr. Hoshi. "How did you do that?"

"I . . . I don't know." Dr. Hoshi stared at her palm, which had returned to normal.

Alex leaped up and sprinted for the swords, the two spear-wielding sentries in pursuit.

"Oh, no, you don't." Supergirl rolled onto her hands and knees.

With the kryptonite-laden swords now several yards away, some of her life force had returned. Enough, at least, for her to use her freeze breath on the sentries' togas. With a frosty crackle, the fabric stiffened, tripping them up.

Alex skirted around the sentries and returned with both swords now firmly nestled in their sheaths.

"Here, can you take these?" Alex held the weapons out to Dr. Hoshi, who was still gawking at her hand.

"Dr. Hoshi? Are you okay?" Supergirl asked, earning a panicked look from the doctor.

"I'm a crossing guard in my free time. This could be really bad!" She held her palm up for the Danvers sisters to see, and they both ducked.

"Whoa! Okay, let's occupy those," said Alex, placing a sword in each of the doctor's hands, "with these." She glanced at Supergirl. "And we need to go now. Can you move?"

With Alex's help, Supergirl staggered to her feet, studying the wound on her leg. It would take a couple of hours to heal, but she still had *one* good leg to stand on. "We should stay. The swords can't hurt me anymore. And I don't run from a fight."

Alex smiled at her sweetly. "You don't have to run. I'm going to carry you."

Alex hoisted Supergirl over one shoulder.

Supergirl sighed. "Dr. Hoshi, can you throw that cloak over me?"

The last thing National City needed was to see their superhero incapacitated.

Right before Dr. Hoshi tossed the cloak over her head, Supergirl glanced at the two statues of Marcus. A third Marcus stood between them.

He grinned at Supergirl and winked.

5

WHILE SUPERGIRL APPRECIATED Alex's help, she was glad that her sister quickly tired from carrying her.

"I don't . . . get it," Alex panted as Supergirl slid off her back. "You were . . . way easier to lift . . . when we were kids."

"I've eaten a lot of pot stickers since then," Supergirl reminded her. "But it's fine. I can walk, Alex," she said. "Better yet, I can *fly*. With all of us." She gestured to Dr. Hoshi, whose eyes widened.

"Up there?" asked Dr. Hoshi, pointing to the sky. "Without a parachute?"

Supergirl grinned. "It's not so bad. Just remember to keep your mouth closed when we take off."

Dr. Hoshi nodded. "Because the rapid intake of air could damage my internal organs."

"And to keep the bugs out of your teeth," said Alex.

"Ready?" Supergirl held an arm out to Dr. Hoshi, who reluctantly inched closer.

"I really don't like flying." Dr. Hoshi shut her eyes and clung to Supergirl's left side.

"You get used to it," Supergirl promised, motioning for Alex to grab hold from the right.

Supergirl sprang into the air, and Dr. Hoshi screamed like a boiling teakettle. Alex laughed as the wind whipped through her hair, and Supergirl laughed along with her.

There was nothing quite like flying.

Up here, Supergirl was untouchable, above all the problems of the world, including her own. She didn't need a fancy MIT diploma or a shelf of sports trophies or the ability to splice DNA. Up here, she was enough. She was free to be herself. She . . .

She was starting to feel a little weak.

Supergirl's forehead broke out in a sweat.

Maybe taking on two passengers after kryptonite exposure wasn't such a good idea.

She blinked and shook her head, tightening her grip on Alex and Dr. Hoshi. Supergirl decreased her speed and flew closer to the tops of the buildings.

"Kara!" Alex shouted into her ear. "Are you OK?"

She nodded tersely, but at that moment, her right biceps spasmed, and she lost her grip on Alex.

Thankfully, Alex had wrapped both *her* arms around Supergirl and only slid a few inches. Still, when Supergirl glanced at her sister, Alex's face was stark white.

"Touch down! Now!" Alex pointed to a roof below them, but Supergirl shook her head.

She was too close to give up.

It took all she had to keep them airborne, and as Supergirl reached the DEO's roof, her strength finally gave out. Instead of making a soft landing, the three women tumbled forward and skidded across the concrete.

Several groans and swear words followed.

Supergirl was the first to recover, and she crawled over to Dr. Hoshi and Alex.

"Are you guys OK? I'm so sorry!"

Dr. Hoshi rolled onto her back and frowned. "You get used to *this?*"

There was an awkward silence. Then all three women burst out laughing. It was a glad-to-be-alive giddiness that ended in more groans and cursing as their injuries were fully felt.

"I'm so sorry," Supergirl repeated. "The kryptonite weakened me more than I thought."

"Then you need to lie down and soak up the sun's energy," said Dr. Hoshi, back in physician mode.

Supergirl hesitated, but did as she was told.

Alex slowly shifted to a crouch, wincing before she stood up. "I'm gonna go downstairs and find J'onn. Dr. Hoshi, will you keep an eye on my sister?"

"Of course." Dr. Hoshi flashed a bloodied elbow at Alex. "Could you bring some water and a first aid k . . . whatever you can find that resembles bandages and gauze?"

Alex nodded and disappeared through the roof access door.

Dr. Hoshi glanced at the laceration on Supergirl's leg. "You seem to already be recovering, but let's check some vitals."

She leaned over and pulled one of Supergirl's eyes open wide. Supergirl flinched, remembering the blast of light Dr. Hoshi had shot from that same hand just minutes before. At Supergirl's reaction, Dr. Hoshi seemed to remember, too, and jerked her hand back.

"Sorry!" she said. "I forgot that . . ." She shook her head. "I have a superpower now, which is crazy. Yesterday, I was a plain old doctor."

"'Plain old'?" Supergirl laughed. "You're an amazing physician who heals humans *and* aliens, not to mention your background in astronomy."

Dr. Hoshi waved away the compliment. "That's nothing. Being a *superhero*?" She gestured at Supergirl. "That's a big deal!"

Supergirl snorted. "I'm only a superhero because of the sun." She pointed skyward. "Take that away, and I'm a plain old magazine reporter."

Dr. Hoshi tilted her head to one side. "I never thought of it like that." She smiled. "Thanks! I actually feel better."

Supergirl smiled back, but inside *she* actually felt worse. Minimizing her accomplishments had stirred up her own self-doubt again.

"So . . . um . . . how do you think you got your superpower?" she asked Dr. Hoshi.

"I'm pretty sure Caesar's Comet was involved. That blast hit me straight on, and if Marcus could use it to create this"—Dr. Hoshi gestured around them—"who knows what else that comet was capable of?" Dr. Hoshi touched two fingers to Supergirl's wrist and counted to herself. "But honestly, I'm not sure I *want* this power. If I can even use it again."

Supergirl's mouth slipped into a mischievous smile. "We can find out." She propped herself on her elbows and glanced around.

Leaning against the wall near the roof's hatch door were a few burlap sacks. At one point they'd been plastic bags full of salt for deicing the roof.

Supergirl pointed to one of the bags. "Try to hit that."

Dr. Hoshi's eyes widened but then crinkled into a smile. "OK."

She raised a hand and flicked it in the direction of the salt bag.

Nothing happened.

Dr. Hoshi flicked her wrist again.

Supergirl frowned. "Try tightening your wrist."

Dr. Hoshi's forehead wrinkled in concentration as she stiffened her wrist and thrust her hand out.

Still nothing.

Dr. Hoshi lowered her arm. "I guess it was a one-time thing," she said.

Supergirl smiled sympathetically. "But your frown answers the question of whether you really wanted that power."

"I guess it does," Dr. Hoshi said with a rueful chuckle. "I don't suppose it matters right now, anyway." She sat next to Supergirl. "We've got bigger problems . . . like being trapped in Ancient Rome."

"Things will return to normal," Supergirl promised her. Remembering what the sentry had said, she added, "The curse *can* be reversed."

"How?" Dr. Hoshi picked gravel out of one of her scraped palms. "That guy you're up against, Marcus—he has kryptonite swords, right?"

"*Had*," Supergirl corrected, pointing across the roof to where the sheathed swords had fallen.

"But who knows how many other tricks he has up his sleeve?" continued Dr. Hoshi. "He knew your secret identity, which means someone inside the organization might be helping him." She leaned closer to Supergirl. "He could have spies everywhere."

The roof hatch door whipped open, and both women jumped. Dr. Hoshi threw her hand out protectively, but it didn't blast anything.

Instead, a bubble of white light enveloped Supergirl and the doctor.

"What the—?" Supergirl extended a hand, and the curve of the bubble shifted with it.

At the same time, Alex stepped through the roof hatch and tossed a roll of linen to Dr. Hoshi. "Found some bandages!"

The linen bounced off the bubble and rolled back toward Alex, who looked from the bandage to the bubble with raised eyebrows.

Dr. Hoshi breathed an audible sigh of relief as J'onn joined Alex. "It's just you guys."

She dropped her hand and instantly, the bubble disappeared.

"OK, I did *not* know she could do that Glinda the Good Witch thing," Alex told J'onn.

They hurried over to Supergirl and Dr. Hoshi, who was marveling at her hands again.

"Supergirl, are you all right?" J'onn asked.

She nodded. "Thanks to Alex and Dr. Hoshi . . . or should I say Dr. Light?" She smirked. "You wanted one superpower. Now you have two."

"But what did I just do?" asked Dr. Hoshi.

"If I had to guess, I'd say you created a force field," said J'onn. "Made of light, as Supergirl pointed out. More important, how did you gain this power?"

Dr. Hoshi held out her arm so Alex could clean and bandage it. "I think it came from the same comet that Marcus used to transform National City."

"By the way, he also stole kryptonite from somewhere," Supergirl informed J'onn, gesturing to her injured leg.

He nodded. "Alex filled me in. I'm having Agent Vasquez inventory *our* alien artifacts in the subbasement to see if anything is missing."

Supergirl shook her head. "I doubt that my blood sample and the kryptonite were recent thefts. He probably stole things while he had the power to turn invisible. Since he no longer can, I think we're safe in that respect." She looked up at J'onn and Alex. "By the way, Dr. Hoshi made a good point earlier. We don't know what else Marcus has up his sleeve—or how his curse works in order to reverse it."

"It's too bad we can't zip in and out of his estate undetected," said Alex.

"We could definitely use a Flash on this Earth," agreed Supergirl, thinking of her friend Barry Allen.

Barry was the fastest man alive on an alternate version of Earth. Supergirl had visited it once using a portal created by Barry's best friend at S.T.A.R. Labs, Cisco Ramon. And before Supergirl went home, Cisco had given her—

"The interdimensional extrapolator!" Supergirl jumped to her feet and winced, remembering her leg injury. She rose a few inches into the air to keep her weight off of it.

J'onn, Alex, and Dr. Hoshi exchanged puzzled looks.

"The what, now?" asked Alex.

"Remember when I went to Barry's Earth and helped him fight aliens?" Supergirl floated in front of her DEO teammates. "Before I left, his friend Cisco gave me a device, an interdimensional extrapolator. It can open a portal between our Earths or let me talk to them if I ever need help!"

"Well, we definitely need help," said J'onn.

"But wouldn't that device be modern tech?" asked Dr. Hoshi. "Marcus's curse would've antiquated it."

Supergirl shook her head. "No! J'onn made me think of it when he mentioned the alien tech in the subbasement. None of that aged, because it's not of this Earth, just like

J'onn and Mon-El and I didn't transform into Ancient Romans, because *we're* not of this Earth."

J'onn smiled and crossed his arms. "And Cisco's device isn't of *this* Earth, either."

Supergirl grinned. "Exactly!"

Alex grabbed Supergirl's arm and pulled her down to the roof. "Okay, so where is this . . . inter . . . galactic . . . planetary . . . whatever?" she asked, fumbling to remember the words.

"The interdimensional extrapolator. At my apartment," said Supergirl. "I can fly there and be back like *that.*" She snapped her fingers.

J'onn nodded. "Do so, but be careful. Marcus may have set traps for you."

"I can go with her," offered Alex.

"Actually," said a voice from the roof hatch door, "I was hoping you could stay."

For the second time, a glowing bubble surrounded Dr. Hoshi and Supergirl, but now it included Alex and J'onn, too.

Everyone turned, and Supergirl saw Alex's girlfriend, Maggie, peek around the roof hatch. "It's just me! Don't explode!"

"OK, people have *got* to stop popping through that door," said Dr. Hoshi as the shield dissolved.

Maggie gestured at her. "What the—?"

"Photon shield," said Alex casually, giving Maggie a quick kiss. "How's the city looking?"

"OK for now," said Maggie. "The police force we *do* have is walking a beat, and people are behaving themselves. But I'm worried things will get worse once the sun goes down."

Alex winced. "Because we don't have streetlights anymore."

"Or police cars with spotlights or even cars with headlights," added Maggie. She smirked. "So here's where I ask for the favor that the DEO owes NCPD from the supercitizen battle. The chief is wondering if you guys could spare any agents to help patrol at night." She cleared her throat. "Specifically, any agents named Supergirl."

Supergirl pressed her lips together. She didn't really have time, but she couldn't abandon her city, either. She just had to hope that Barry could come through for her.

She nodded to Maggie. "Of course. I'll keep my ears open."

"And we'll give whatever else we can," said J'onn.

Maggie pressed her hands together. "Thank you. I'll go tell the chief."

Alex glanced up at the sun. "And *I* should probably tell the agents to get some rest so they can be fresh for tonight."

J'onn put a hand on her shoulder. "You should rest, too. You've been through a lot."

"So has Kara." Alex gestured to Supergirl. "But she's going back out there."

"I don't have much choice," Supergirl told her sister. "Don't worry. I'll be fine. Just get rid of those things." She pointed to the kryptonite-infused swords. "I'll be back at sunset."

Without waiting for further argument from Alex, she zipped off the roof and across town, hovering above her apartment building. It was the first time she'd seen it since National City had transformed. Ordinarily, it was much taller, but now it was only five stories, and she feared that the other floors might not truly be inside.

Supergirl landed softly on the roof and tentatively entered through the hatch. When she stepped into the building, a placard on the wall revealed the correct floor. With a relieved sigh, she zipped down the stairwell to her apartment and ran to the bathroom.

Then she ran right back out.

"Gross, gross, gross!"

Her porcelain toilet had been replaced by a wooden contraption that looked like a step stool with a hole in it. And where the toilet paper holder had been, a stick with a sea sponge tied to it leaned against the wall.

"No *way* I'm using that thing," she declared.

Supergirl glanced around her living room and spotted a

roll of parchment with "*CatCo* magazine" burned into one corner.

"This wasn't a great issue anyway." She ripped off a sizable piece and headed for the bathroom.

When she stepped out a couple of minutes later, she vowed to drink as little water as possible over the next few days. If her private toilet was like this, she didn't even want to think about using a public one.

Supergirl walked to her bedroom and opened a chest drawer. She reached beneath various objects inside until she found what she was looking for: a round, palm-sized piece of metal accented with three triangular points.

Supergirl pulled out the interdimensional extrapolator and grinned.

The last time she'd used it, a quick press of a button at its center had opened a portal between Earth 1, where Barry lived, and Earth 38, where she was. But she didn't want to risk exposing another Earth to Marcus just yet. Not until after she'd talked to Barry.

"Let's see what happens when I do *this*." Supergirl held the button down for several beats, and a flash of blue light emanated from the extrapolator. Instead of creating a portal, though, it created a small window through which she could see a laboratory.

Supergirl's heart pounded faster. "Hello?" she called.

"Hello?" a female voice responded from out of her sight line. "Who's there?"

"Uh, it's . . . it's Supergirl," she said, trying to place the voice of the other woman. "I'm friends with Ba . . . with Flash."

"Supergirl?!" There was a rapid shuffle of footsteps, and then a sunny face appeared opposite hers. "Oh, my God! Kara! It's so good to see you!"

Supergirl grinned from ear to ear and waved. "It's good to see you, too, Iris."

6

UPERGIRL FELT ALMOST GIDDY WITH relief, and her cheeks began to ache from grinning so hard. "So . . . we're talking across universes!"

"Yeah, what . . . how . . ." Iris West shook her head, laughing. "I still can't believe it!"

"I know!" Supergirl replied. "How've you been?"

The last time Supergirl had seen Barry's fiancée and S.T.A.R. Labs teammate, they'd all been trapped in the Music Meister's twisted reality. He'd sent them into a 1940s movie musical to deal with their personal problems, and the only way out was to give the movie a happy ending.

"I've been great! You?" Iris's smile slipped a little. "Oh, wait. You're trying to reach Barry through an interdimensional window. Probably *not* so great, huh?"

"It's been a challenging couple of days," Supergirl admitted with a smile. "Is Barry around? I could use his speed for something."

Iris sucked in her breath and frowned. "Aw, sorry. He's actually on Earth 2 right now."*

Supergirl's shoulders slumped, and she tapped her forehead, thinking. Iris had a younger brother, Wally, who had superspeed like Barry's, but Supergirl wasn't sure he was ready to go up against Marcus if it came to that.

"Is there anything I can do to help?" Iris asked.

"Unfortunately, I don't think so," said Supergirl. "We're up against a guy who summoned some demons, and I need to know how he did it."

Iris's eyebrows practically disappeared into her hairline. "Demons? As in *demon* demons?"

Supergirl nodded. "Beelzebub and Tempus Fugit, to be exact," she said.

Iris whistled under her breath. "And there wasn't anything about them on the Internet?"

Supergirl glanced around her antiquated room. "Our Internet is . . . down right now."

"Well, I could look them up for you," said Iris with a shrug. "Hang on a second."

She walked away from the window and returned holding a laptop. Supergirl watched Iris's fingers fly across the keys.

*Read all about The Flash's adventures in *The Flash: Johnny Quick.*

"Wow. You're as fast as Flash on that thing," Supergirl commented.

Iris grinned. "I do a lot of typing at *Picture News.*"

Supergirl's forehead wrinkled. "The *Central City Picture News*?" She and Iris might be from different Earths, but their versions of cities were similar. "You write for the newspaper?"

Iris nodded, studying her laptop's screen. "I'm an investigative journalist."

Supergirl's jaw dropped. "Me, too! I mean, my alter ego is. For CatCo Worldwide Media."

Iris glanced up. "Ha! Small world . . . s."

They both laughed.

Supergirl watched Iris work for a moment. "Do you ever wonder if what you're doing is . . . enough?"

Iris frowned. "What do you mean?"

"Like . . . if being a journalist is important enough."

"I think words have a lot of power," said Iris. "And it's better that they come from us than someone who would use them for evil." She smiled again. "I'm protecting the people of my city that way. Like a superhero with a laptop."

"And awesome fashion sense," added Supergirl. She felt slightly relieved. Maybe when they reversed the curse and she got back to CatCo, she could make more of a difference there as well.

Iris laughed. "What about you? I see some off-the-shoulder dresses hanging up in the background."

"For really special occasions." Supergirl didn't want to tell her that they were actually stolas that smelled faintly of farm animal. "Were you able to find anything on the demons?"

Iris held up her screen so Supergirl could see it. "I found a couple of books that might help. They're translated from ancient texts. Maybe you could check your local library for them?"

If the library's still standing, Supergirl thought. But she glanced at the book titles and then turned her gaze to a blank wall and scored the titles into the stone with her heat vision.

"Thanks, Iris," she said. "Tell Barry I said hi."

"We're always here if you need us, Kara." Iris winked, then vanished as Supergirl closed the interdimensional window.

"I hope I'll always be here for you, too," she said in a soft voice.

Supergirl glanced out her window; the sun was low in the sky. She maybe had a couple of hours until she had to be back at the DEO. She turned and surveyed her collection of stolas.

"Should I go for cream, cream, or . . . maybe cream?" she asked herself before selecting one and slipping it on.

This version of her Kara guise definitely wasn't as colorful as her modern clothing, but as she twirled around and studied her stola, she had to admit it was pretty comfortable. She pulled her hair into a ponytail and tied it in place with a strip of leather.

"And now . . . glasses," she said to herself with a frown.

She wasn't a history buff, but she was pretty sure the Ancient Romans didn't have eyewear. Yet glasses were paramount to her disguise.

Opening her jewelry box, she removed a pair of hoop earrings and a coiled bracelet. Then she grabbed a clear bottle from the kitchen counter. After some metal-bending with her superstrength and glass-cutting with her laser vision, Kara tried on the final product.

"Let's see what we've got." She picked up a mirror and nodded at her reflection. "I. Look. Ridiculous."

But she also looked nothing like Supergirl.

Tucking her costume into a leather satchel, Kara hurried out of her building and through the busy streets. Next stop, the library.

As soon as Kara walked into the lobby, she froze.

On an average day, the National City Library had, maybe, twenty people or so browsing the shelves, and a few college students sitting at the research tables. Today, the place was as crowded as an amusement park.

A throng was gathered around the librarian's station, requesting books . . . or, rather, scrolls. All the seats in the research area were taken, so some people sprawled out on the floor. One of them, a dark-haired woman, sat in a lotus pose while her eyes darted from one edge of a scroll to the other.

Kara ran toward her. "Lena!"

Lena looked around, and her eyes lit up. "Kara!" She uncrossed her legs and scrambled to her feet, throwing her arms around her friend. "Thank God you're all right! I went by your place this morning, but you weren't there."

"I've been busy trying to figure out what's going on," Kara said.

"Me, too!" said Lena. "I don't think my mother's behind whatever happened, but I can't imagine who else *would* be. I mean, to cast such an elaborate illusion."

Lillian Luthor, Lena's adoptive mother, directed Cadmus, a research project with a goal to destroy all alien life on Earth. Normally Kara might agree with Lena's suspicions, but not this time.

"It's not—" She glanced at the other people nearby and pulled Lena away. "It's not an illusion," she whispered. "A very twisted person put a curse on the city."

"A curse?" Lena let out an airy laugh. "Kara, there's no such thing as curses. No, this is the result of some hallucinogen pumped into the atmosphere. I just need to find the antidote."

"Lena." Kara gripped her shoulders. "This is all very real. Supergirl told me." She held up a piece of parchment on which she'd scrawled the book—scroll—titles. "And the key to reversing it is somewhere in these scrolls." Kara turned to the shelves around them. "I just have to find that answer."

Lena studied Kara. "You're serious, aren't you?"

"I wish I wasn't," said Kara. "But if we don't reverse this soon, we'll be stuck like this forever."

Lena sighed and stared at the ceiling. "Will we ever have a normal week?"

"I think bad guys *maybe* take Christmas off," Kara said with a smile.

Lena held out a hand. "Could I see the titles?"

Kara passed her the parchment. "If the library has them, I think they'll be in the religion section." She eyed the librarian's desk, which still hosted a crowd. "But I don't have much time."

"Luckily for you, I've been here all day, so I know this place backward and forward." Lena pointed to a staircase in the center of the room. "We want the second-floor stacks."

When Lena said "stacks," she meant it literally. The shelves were no longer lined with orderly rows of books but were crammed with scrolls that threatened to spill onto the floor. Lena eased a random scroll out of a stack and glanced at it.

"We're close. What we want should be a couple more shelves over."

She and Kara continued down the aisle, and Lena plucked another scroll from a pile. She put it back and crouched, searching the ones beneath it.

"Aha!" She pulled out a stack of scrolls and handed them to Kara.

"Which of these is the right book?" asked Kara.

Lena grinned. "All of them. Every scroll is a different section."

They settled on the floor, and each unrolled one of the scrolls.

"What are we looking for, exactly?" asked Lena.

"Any mention of the demons Beelzebub or Tempus Fugit," said Kara. "And the rituals used to summon them."

Lena opened her mouth, as if to ask a question, then closed it and got to work.

For the next half hour, there were sighs and rustles of parchment as they reviewed the scrolls.

Finally, Kara found a scroll entitled *Demons to Do Thy Bidding.*

"I think I've got something." Her finger zipped across the passages in the scroll until they fell upon *Tempus Fugit.* "This is it!"

Lena peered over her shoulder, and they read together.

Summon Tempus Fugit at thy peril. He will give much but take in kind. Life for life, death for death.

"City for city," Kara mumbled.

To summon Tempus Fugit, consecrate the altar using the blood and spirit of a champion.

"Blood and spirit?" Lena wrinkled her nose, and Kara nodded.

"Supergirl's blood. But I don't understand the spirit part. I don't feel any—I mean, *Supergirl* said she didn't feel any different," Kara corrected herself.

Lena rested against a wall, legs stretched out in front of her. "Maybe it refers to something else."

"Maybe. But what?" Kara skimmed the scroll. "Here's the info on Beelzebub! The ritual's about the same." She rolled up the scroll and got to her feet. "I have to get this to Supergirl." Kara leaned over and hugged Lena. "Thank you for your help."

"Anytime." Lena smiled up at her. "I'll be here if you need me."

Kara nodded and draped the satchel over her shoulder. She sprinted down the stairs, pushing her way through a crowd that was growing as the sun set. With no electronics at home to entertain them, people were finally willing to read again.

And all it took was a curse, Kara thought wryly.

She made her way to a nearby alley and took off into the sky, landing a few minutes later on the DEO balcony, where her sister was watching the city.

"You're early." Alex smirked and pointed to Kara's glasses. "And those spectacles . . . are a spectacle."

"Hey, be nice!" Kara removed her glasses and smacked her sister's arm with them. "I made them myself."

Alex hid a smile. "I never would've guessed. Were you able to reach Barry?"

"No, but I still have good news." She grabbed Alex's hand and hurried inside and down the steps. "J'onn!"

The DEO director rounded a corner with Mon-El and Dr. Hoshi.

"Hey!" Mon-El embraced Kara. "I heard you ran into trouble earlier."

"Nothing me and my squad couldn't handle." She smiled at Alex and Dr. Hoshi.

"You wanted to see me, Miss Danvers?" J'onn prompted.

"Yes!" Kara reached into her satchel and pulled out the library scroll. "I found out how Marcus got us into this mess." She pointed out the passage.

"'To summon Tempus Fugit, you consecrate the altar, using the blood and spirit of a champion,'" read Alex. "Gross."

"But I still *have* my spirit," said Kara.

J'onn shook his head. "Spirit can mean soul, but it can also mean life force . . . breath. Did Marcus ever steal your breath?"

Kara shrugged. "He probably had plenty of chances when I was unconscious."

"But he would have needed it to start the curse," Alex reminded them. She snapped her fingers. "And he did kiss you that one time!"

Kara clapped a hand over her mouth.

Back when the citizens had gained superpowers, Marcus had stopped Kara from being pulverized by a truck. He'd stolen a kiss from her as his reward.

And apparently, he'd also stolen her breath.

"That sleazy jerk." Kara wiped at her mouth, as if the unwanted kiss had just happened.

"I hate that guy a little more each day," said Mon-El.

"OK, so, to reverse the curse, we just need to get Kara's blood and breath back," said Alex.

J'onn frowned. "I have a feeling it won't be that easy."

"On TV shows, reversing a curse takes a counter-curse," Dr. Hoshi chimed in. She gazed off into the distance. "Man, I miss TV."

Alex tapped the scroll. "Let's keep reading. Maybe the counter-curse is in here."

But even with five of them looking, they couldn't find anything that would help.

"This is pointless!" Kara dropped the scroll onto the table. "Even if we knew the counter-curse, there's probably a specific ritual for *that*. This isn't our area of expertise."

"What we need is a demonologist," said J'onn. "But that's usually a religious official."

"And anyone official in this city seems to be working for Marcus," said Alex.

Kara reached into her satchel again. "Luckily, I have connections outside the city!" She held up the interdimensional extrapolator and pressed the button. "I've already talked to Iris West on this thing, and in just a couple seconds, we'll be"—the interdimensional window opened into a room with a fountain at its center and frescoes on the walls—"invading someone's home. Huh." She frowned and flipped the extrapolator over. "I did not know this thing had different location settings."

"Oh, it doesn't." A familiar, unwelcome face appeared in front of the window.

"Marcus," Kara said, frowning.

"Hello, everyone." He wiggled his fingertips at them. "Why the sour faces?" He pointed at Mon-El. "Ugh. Yours is particularly ghastly! Did you eat a bag of lemons?"

Mon-El turned to Kara. "I'd really like to make him eat his own sandals. Please?"

Kara shushed him. "What did you do to my extrapolator?" she asked Marcus.

"I was hurt that you'd go to someone else with your troubles." He pouted and pressed a hand to his heart. "So I used a little magic to make your device route directly to my receiving room." He grinned rakishly at her. "Oh, and I've blocked its ability to create portals. Can't have you popping in to kill me in my sleep. *Or* make me eat my own sandals." He shook a finger at Mon-El.

With an annoyed grunt, Kara pressed the extrapolator button again, and Marcus disappeared.

"Well, at least now we know he can be killed," said Alex.

"We're not killing anyone," said Kara.

"But we do need to find a demonologist," said J'onn, "even if it means knocking on every door in this city."

"I can help with that, sir." Agent Vasquez approached the conference table. She smiled apologetically. "Sorry for the interruption, but I have the inventory of alien artifacts." She handed a scroll to J'onn, who reviewed it with Kara reading over one shoulder.

"Everything seems to be accounted for," J'onn said with a nod.

"Would you like me to assemble a team to start searching for demonologists?" Vasquez asked.

"Actually"—Kara held up a finger—"before we do that, I think we should talk to Winn and see what he's found out."

"Winn?" Alex repeated with a frown. "But he and James are outside the dome, and we're *in*side."

"Not for long." Kara took the scroll from J'onn and turned it so the others could see. "I think it's time we bring our boys home."

7

RUSTLE, RUSTLE. CRINKLE.

Winn's ears perked up at the sound and he narrowed his eyes at James as they pulled away from yet another occultist's shop. They'd been to four so far, and none had held anything promising. But that hadn't stopped Winn from picking up a trinket at each location.

"I hear you pawing through my stuff, Olsen," Winn said. "Hands off the merch."

"Why do you need all this junk, anyway?" James pulled a gnarled chicken foot from a paper bag.

"When we first started crime-fighting, we were only up against aliens and evil inventors," said Winn. "But then, if you'll remember, my ex-girlfriend went a li'l cray-cray from a curse."

"Turning into Silver Banshee," James acknowledged with a nod.

"*That* was when we should've started learning about magic." Winn smacked a palm against the steering wheel for emphasis. "If we had, we might've seen the Rome Dome coming."

"This?" James gestured to a Roman building as they drove past. "I don't think anyone could've seen this coming, man."

"Well, we might've been better prepared to deal with it, at least," amended Winn. From the driver's-side window, he spotted a store with garish magenta curtains. "Now that we've seen *two* cases of curses, something tells me more might be coming."

Winn glanced back at the shop curtains. They were decorated with moons and stars . . . and a familiar yet strange symbol.

"I guess you're right," said James. "We can't avoid it, so we might as well steer into the skid."

Winn slammed on the brakes, and the van skidded several feet. James shouted in surprise, and Winn hunched his shoulders, giving his friend a lopsided smile. "Sorry. That was a ridiculously well-timed coincidence."

James loosened his seat belt, scowling. "Mind telling me why I just left my stomach in the back of the van?"

Winn pointed out the window. "Look at the curtains on that storefront."

James followed Winn's finger and pointed one of his own. "Hey, that's one of the symbols from the music hall's roof!"

Winn nodded and reached for his door handle. "Wanna check it out? Fifth time's a charm."

"I'm down." James held out the chicken foot. "Should we rub it for luck?"

Winn smirked. "Wasn't very lucky for the chicken."

They hopped out of the van and approached the store entrance. A banner above the door announced the shop as NIMUE'S PARLOR TRICKS.

A set of bells jangled above the door as they entered, but nobody arrived to greet them.

"Hello?" called Winn.

To his left was a tall wooden cabinet filled with candles and incense sticks in various colors. Winn sniffed an incense stick and recoiled.

"OK. Somebody's replicated the smell inside our van."

James chuckled and strolled farther into the store. "Hello?" he called out. "Paying customers here."

"Maybe whoever runs the shop is out to dinner," suggested Winn, following James. He paused at a bookshelf and started pulling out anything that sounded promising.

"*Warly's Wizardry, Non-Metal Alchemy* . . . aha!" He nabbed a yellow book with symbols on the spine. "*Demonology for Dummies.* Man, they make these books about *everything*."

Winn flipped to the first page, which held a massive warning in bold black letters.

"'Summoning circles must be closed and incantations must be accurate,'" he read aloud. "'Otherwise your soul . . . belongs to the demon'"—he frowned—"'to be tortured for eternity.'"

"Demon?" James popped up beside him, and Winn yelped, fumbling with the book.

"Dude, you cannot sneak up on someone in an occult shop!" Winn laid the book on a counter to peruse.

James smirked. "Sorry, man. I didn't know you were scared of this stuff."

Winn narrowed his eyes. "I'm not scared. I'm danger-aware." He thumbed through the pages until he found one of the symbols they'd been looking for. "'Beelzebub. The demon of vessels,'" read Winn.

"Vessels? Like ships?" asked James.

Winn shook his head. "I think it's more like . . . human vessels. Whoever cursed the city must have needed more power. Demon power." He shuddered and searched for the next symbol.

"There it is. Tempus Fugit," said James, pointing out a page.

"The demon of time. Makes sense," said Winn. He ran his index finger down the passage while he read. "Looks like the summoning requires the blood and breath of a champion."

"Kara," James whispered. He and Winn exchanged a look. "She's probably okay, right?"

"If she wasn't, things would look a lot worse in the Rome Dome," Winn pointed out then returned to the text.

"There's an incantation to summon Tempus Fugit." Winn tapped the page. "And one to banish him."

"That's a whole lotta words for 'Get out.'" James squinted at the text. "Ex . . . exeee? Ex ayyy? Exeatis, Tempus—"

Winn snapped the book shut and clapped a hand over James's mouth. "Are you crazy?" he whispered.

James brushed him off. "*What* is your problem?"

"If we don't perform the ritual perfectly, our souls belong to the demon." Winn glanced around nervously. "And there's torture involved. You've seen me get a paper cut. I am *not* built for torture!"

James rubbed his temples and sighed. "Fine. But if *we* don't recite the incantation, who's going to do it?"

Winn opened the book again. "I don't know. A priest? Maybe it says in here."

He flipped to the section on Tempus Fugit and found the page James had been reading.

Except now a yellow sticky note covered the incantations.

On it, two words had been written: *Jason Blood.*

Every hair on Winn's body stood on end, and, beside him, James sucked in his breath.

"Was that . . . uh . . . was that there a minute ago?" James pointed at the sticky note.

"No." Winn's voice came out as a squeak. He cleared his throat. "No, it was not."

They both took a giant step away from the counter.

"It's cool. I'm not scared," said James, swallowing hard. "I'm danger-aware."

"Speak for yourself," Winn said in a breathless whisper. "If a black cat jumps out or I hear a thunderclap, there's gonna be a Winn-shaped hole in that door." He pointed to the exit.

But nothing crossed their path except sunlight, and the only sound came from traffic outside.

Winn and James relaxed and stepped closer to the book.

"So who's Jason Blood?" asked James.

"You mean apart from a guy with a very unfortunate last name?" Winn did a quick search for Jason Blood on his phone. It resulted in a list of websites from prestigious colleges and museums, as well as images of a man whose auburn hair was accented by a white streak. Most websites referenced his knowledge of ancient civilizations and . . .

"You're not gonna believe this," said Winn. He held up his phone for James to see. "Jason Blood is an expert on demons. A demonologist, to be exact."

James's eyebrows went up. "Just what we're looking for."

Winn glanced at the ceiling. "Thank you, Occult Shop Fairy!" he called with a little wave. He reached into his wallet and pulled out some money, putting it on the counter. "We're gonna buy this book and go now!" He tugged at James's arm and headed for the exit.

"You don't want to stay in case we need more help?" James asked teasingly.

Winn waited until they were on the street with the door closed behind them before answering. "I didn't want to press our luck. Nobody does favors without expecting something in return. And who knows what a restless spirit might have in mind?"

James shuddered and pushed Winn toward the van. "Good point. So how do we get in touch with this Jason Blood?"

"E-mail, of course." Winn climbed into the van and grabbed his laptop. He pulled up Jason's business networking account, typed a quick message, and pressed Send. "Fingers crossed that he sees it and—" Winn's e-mail dinged with a new message. "That was freakishly fast."

He refreshed his e-mail and groaned.

The new message was an auto-reply from Jason Blood.

"'Thank you for your interest,'" Winn read aloud. "'I'm on a speaking tour for the next three months and will respond to all correspondence upon my return.'" Winn blew a raspberry at the laptop screen. "So much for Jason *Dud*."

"Where's he touring?" asked James. "Maybe it's close by."

Winn clicked on a link in Jason's e-mail signature and searched his website. "Oh, ho, ho! You are not wrong, my friend." He smiled at James. "He's here in National City every night this week!"

"Great!" James clapped his hands. "Wait." He frowned. "Which part of National City?"

Winn clicked on another link and fake-cried.

Jason Blood was speaking at National City Music Hall.

Which had been changed into the palace with demonic symbols on the roof.

"We can't get to him," Winn muttered. "He's in the Rome Dome."

"But so are Kara, Alex, J'onn, and Mon-El," James pointed out. "Maybe they'll find him."

Winn sat up straight. "We can't count on that. I need to come up with a way to reach them."

James glanced at the setting sun. "How long will that take?"

Winn shrugged. "Days. Weeks. It's not like they're going anywhere."

A police siren sounded somewhere in the distance, and James cleared his throat. "Then while you work on that, maybe I should . . ."

Winn smirked. James didn't even need to finish his sentence. "I think this city needs Guardian more than ever. Suit up. It's going to be a long night."

Supergirl yawned and smacked herself on both cheeks as she leaned against the counter of the control room. It had been a long night.

After she'd told the others her plan to bring Winn and James home, Alex had been gung-ho to begin. Supergirl was just as eager to retrieve her friends but reminded Alex of their biggest challenge.

"It's almost nighttime," she'd said. "Winn and James are probably patrolling the streets right now, and for my plan to work, they need to be at Winn's apartment."

So while they waited for morning, Alex and Mon-El had watched over the prisoners, and Supergirl and J'onn had taken shifts flying over the city, listening and looking for signs of trouble. The one upside to living in an ancient city: there were fewer violent street crimes. Supergirl and the DEO team had broken up several bar fights and foiled a few robberies at knifepoint, but for the most part, the city had been quiet.

When she wasn't patrolling, Supergirl had taken cat-naps on the balcony, but now that the sun was rising, it was time to stay on her feet.

Alex wandered into the control room, yawning, too. "Mon-El just took over my shift. J'onn's still on patrol?"

"Yes, but he should be back soon," said Supergirl. "I guess we should start prepping the device." She motioned for Alex to follow her to the subbasement.

It was lucky that Supergirl had caught a glimpse of the subbasement inventory the day before. She *and* the others had forgotten about a piece of alien tech that had gotten them into and out of some sticky situations. Now it was going to get them out of another one.

"A little help?" asked Alex, patting the subbasement door.

Many of the secure DEO doors had been replaced by extra-heavy stone ones, impossible for the average person to move but easy for Supergirl to drag out of the way. As they stepped into the artifacts room, she whistled at what she saw.

Supergirl had been expecting to see something akin to a police evidence room, with shelves holding boxes of alien tech, like helmets and communicators. Instead, she was standing at the edge of a cavernous expanse that could have housed a personal plane.

"Holy cow, this place is bigger than my apartment!" Her voice echoed off the walls as she gazed around her.

There *were* a few shelves holding small tech items, but most of the room was filled with laser cannons and other high-tech weaponry and armor.

Alex smirked, pointing to the opposite wall, where a giant metallic archway had been stowed. "Look familiar?"

The transmatter portal.

Roulette, an evil yet entrepreneurial woman, had built it to send humans to Slaver's Moon, but Supergirl had destroyed it with her heat vision. When the DEO confiscated it, however, Winn repaired it, and the team had later used it for a rescue mission aboard a Daxamite ship. As long as someone had the coordinates of where they needed to go, it could take them there in a heartbeat.

"That's it!" Supergirl tugged her sister's hand and ran across the room. "Let's clear the area."

She pushed aside a table laden with body armor and a barrel with strange writing on it.

"Is all this stuff from Fort Rozz?" Supergirl rolled the barrel away with the tips of her fingers.

"Not all," J'onn said as he entered the room. "Some items we took from visiting aliens, per interstellar law, and some we took from people who can't be trusted with so much as a box of cookies." He plucked at a yellow-and-blue suit on the armor table.

"Are we ready to fire this thing up?" Alex asked once the portal area was clear.

Supergirl stepped back and studied the arch. "I think so!" She rubbed her palms together. "Let's do this!"

"Yeah!" cheered Alex.

Nobody moved.

Supergirl faced Alex and J'onn. "Let's try that again." She raised a fist for emphasis. "Let's do this!"

Alex and J'onn glanced at each other.

"I don't know how to use it," said Alex. "My focus is bioengineering."

"Neither do I," said J'onn. "I'm into criminal justice."

They turned to Supergirl, who snorted. "I'm just a reporter. Both of you know *way* more than I do."

Alex gave her a strange look but shook her head. "Then we need help from someone with a high-tech intellect."

Supergirl clapped. "I know the perfect person! Be right back!"

She flew out of the artifacts room, up the stairs, and a few blocks away, zipping into the National City Library, which was all but empty.

"Lena!" she called, flying from floor to floor.

There was no sight or sound of her best friend.

Supergirl left the library and headed for Luthor Corp.

Since Lena's apartment was outside the Ancient Rome boundaries, Supergirl mused, she might be sleeping in her office.

But a quick fly-by revealed no Lena Luthor there, either.

Where could she be? Supergirl wondered to herself. *The temple?*

Supergirl headed in that direction, but a spectacle outside Marcus's estate made her pause.

Dozens—no, *hundreds*—of people thronged the entry gates, forming an untidy line that extended half a city block.

"What are they doing?"

Supergirl swooped low, watching and listening for signs of what was happening.

The people were all well dressed, and as they got closer to Marcus's front door, they preened themselves and fidgeted with the small sacks and covered baskets they were holding.

"Oh, this had better not be some sort of Kiss-Marcus's-Butt line." Supergirl frowned and used her X-ray vision to see inside the sacks and baskets.

Empty. All of them.

So the people were hoping to *get* something from Marcus, not give anything to him. And Marcus would no doubt play the hero.

Throwing caution to the wind, Supergirl shouted, "Lena Luthor!"

The crowd glanced up at her and whispered among themselves. Lena's name passed from person to person until somewhere near the front of the line, the crowd parted, and Lena emerged.

"Supergirl?" she asked with wide eyes. "What are you doing here?"

Supergirl landed beside her. "Kara Danvers said you could help me." She held open an arm. "Will you come?"

"Kara?" Lena repeated, her forehead wrinkling in concern. "Of course." She reached out and put an arm around Supergirl's shoulders, shutting her eyes in preparation for flight.

Supergirl leaped into the air with Lena, speeding back to DEO headquarters and the artifacts room.

"Miss Luthor." J'onn nodded at Lena when they landed.

"Hello, Director Henshaw. Alex." Lena gave a little wave. "Why am I here, exactly?" She turned to Supergirl. "And where *is* here?"

"A secret government facility," Alex said tersely, giving Supergirl a look.

"We need your technical expertise," Supergirl told Lena, pointing to the portal. "Can you make this thing work? Winn operated it once with a laptop, but"—she twisted her hands together—"we don't exactly have access to one right now."

Lena approached the arch. "I'll bet it has a manual override," she said.

While Lena worked, Alex nudged Supergirl. "You flew her here without a blindfold? She already knows more about us than she should!"

"Relax! She had her eyes closed," Supergirl whispered. "And I'm more worried about something else." In a louder voice, she asked, "Lena, what were you doing at Marcus's estate?"

Lena looked up from a panel she was trying to open and glanced across the room at them. "Morning salutations to get food and money, of course!"

Alex pointed at Lena. "And you were there?" She turned toward J'onn and Supergirl. "That doesn't sound like Lena."

"No, but it sounds like an Ancient Roman," Supergirl said with a sigh. "Marcus said the curse would start putting people in an Ancient Roman mind-set. I guess it's started." She glanced at her best friend. "Poor Lena. She'd hate this if she knew."

From across the room, Lena sighed, too, and banged a fist against the portal. "I can't get this cover off!"

"I can rip it open," said Supergirl.

Alex placed a hand on Supergirl's arm. "Let's not destroy our one chance of bringing Winn here." She flagged down an agent passing the open door. "Whitby! Can you bring me a hammer and chisel?"

Whitby paused in the doorway and blinked at her. "Why don't you get them yourself?"

Supergirl, Alex, and J'onn all stared in shock.

"Ex*cuse* me?" said Alex.

"I'm not your servant," said Whitby. "If anything, *you* should be at *my* disposal."

Supergirl saw the fire ignite in her sister's eyes. "Uh-oh."

Alex stormed across the room. "The first time was a request; this will be an order. Bring me a hammer and chisel, Agent Whitby."

Whitby curled his lip at Alex. "Be silent. I don't take orders from a woman."

Alex arched an eyebrow. "Do you take punches from a woman?" She reeled her arm back, but Supergirl grabbed her elbow.

"OK. Let's not do something we'll regret," she said with a light laugh.

"Whitby, get the hammer and chisel," J'onn instructed the agent.

"At your command." Immediately, Whitby hurried away.

Alex whirled on J'onn. "You're going to let him get away with that?"

"Normally, you know I wouldn't," said J'onn. "But did you hear his words? 'Be silent.' 'At your command.' Whitby doesn't speak that formally."

"That's the curse affecting him," Supergirl said. "The same way the curse is affecting . . ." She trailed off and nodded in Lena's direction.

Alex frowned. "Why isn't it affecting me, then? I'm human."

"True," J'onn said with a nod. "But I linked to your mind to understand Latin, and I wasn't affected by the curse. It's possible my psyche's protecting yours."

Agent Whitby returned with a hammer and chisel, presenting them both to J'onn.

"Thank you, Whitby," Alex tried again.

He looked her up and down and left without a word.

"Oh, I'm definitely having a one-on-one with that guy when this is over," Alex grumbled.

J'onn handed the tools to Lena, who smiled gratefully and popped the panel door open.

She stared at the interface, and for a moment, Supergirl worried that Lena might be too influenced by the curse to understand the technology. But Lena pressed a few buttons, and the interior arc of the portal lit up.

"Woo-hoo!" Supergirl cheered and high-fived Lena. "Now we can get Winn and James!"

"Are you one hundred percent sure they'll be there?" asked Alex. "Because if Marcus noticed when you talked to Iris, he'll definitely notice this." She gestured at the portal.

"We've probably only got one shot," J'onn added.

"I know," said Supergirl, "but this attempt will be as good as any."

"I need a latitude and longitude to send you to," said Lena, fingers poised over a keypad.

Alex gave Supergirl a troubled look. "We don't have that information."

"Actually . . ." Supergirl's lips slid into a sly smile, and she turned to Lena. "It's 34.1546° N by . . ." She thought for a moment. "118.3340° W."

Lena punched it in while Alex gawked at Supergirl. "How did you *know* that?"

"What can I say?" Supergirl shrugged and smiled. "There's no place like home."

"It's done," said Lena, stepping back to join them.

With a buzzing crackle, the portal swirled to life, spiraling in purple and white electricity. For a brief second, the electricity settled, and Supergirl glimpsed Winn and James fast asleep in Winn's living room.

"We did it!" she shouted with a triumphant smile, running toward the portal.

"Whoa, whoa, whoa!" Alex grabbed Supergirl's arm. "You can't just jump through there. What if Marcus sees you?"

Supergirl shook her head vehemently. "There's no way he'd close a portal with me on the other side," she said. "But he might before I get there."

Alex considered this for half a second. Then she pushed Supergirl toward the arch. "Go. Go, go, go."

Supergirl leaped into the portal, her body tingling as she passed through, and landed safely on the hardwood floor of Winn's apartment. Both Winn and James awoke with a start and gaped at Supergirl in astonishment.

Then Winn let out a loud whoop.

"YES!!! That is my *girl*!"

He and James scrambled to their feet and tackled Supergirl in a three-person hug.

"You have no idea how good it is to see you guys," she said, squeezing them tightly.

"Ow!"

"Ow! Kara . . ."

She winced and released them. "Right. Superstrong! Forgot. Sorry."

Winn pointed at the portal behind her. "How . . . who . . ."

James nudged him into silence. "We have so much to tell you," he said to Supergirl.

Winn nodded. "Yeah, yeah! We know what happened and who can stop it!"

Supergirl beamed at him. "I was hoping you'd say that." Her expression turned serious. "We only have a few days to set things right, or National City will be stuck in the past forever. I can't make you guys come with me, but—"

James held up a hand. "We're coming. And we'll fix it together. Right, Winn?"

They both glanced at Winn, who was scooping books and tech gadgets into his messenger bag.

He paused and grinned at James and Supergirl. "Oh, just try to stop us."

8

ALEX PACED THE FLOOR IN FRONT of the portal, cracking her knuckles and breathing deeply.

Three minutes had passed since Supergirl had jumped from the DEO headquarters into Winn's apartment. After she'd counted another minute, Alex let out an aggravated growl. "What's taking so long?"

Lena put a hand on Alex's shoulder. "I'm sure everything's fine. Supergirl's proven she can look after herself." She stepped away. "Now, if I'm no longer needed, I must go." Lena bowed her head at J'onn and Alex.

A flicker of surprise crossed J'onn's face, but he bowed

his head, as well. "Thank you for your assistance, Miss Luthor."

"Wait, you're not gonna stick around to see what happens?" Alex asked.

Lena shook her head. "I've already missed this morning's salutation. I don't want to be late to the bathhouse."

Alex recoiled. "You're leaving to take a bath?"

J'onn nudged Alex and whispered, "Remember, Lena's under the curse's influence."

"I know that," she whispered back. "But if Lena's putting a *bath* in front of this crisis, this curse is advancing quickly. Can't you link minds with her?"

"Lena will be safer if Marcus doesn't know she's connected to us," J'onn said.

"I guess you have a point." Alex turned. "Aaand she's gone anyway."

The portal crackled beside them, and Supergirl burst from its center with James and Winn each holding one of her hands.

"Oh, thank God." Alex sighed and hurried over to the trio. "Is everyone all right?" She hugged each of them in turn.

"Of course!" said Supergirl.

"Better now," said James.

"Yeah," said Winn, breaking into song. "Reunited, and it feels so go-oo-od!"

The others laughed, and Alex smirked. "You realize that's a love song."

"Pshhht," Winn scoffed, then rubbed his ear. "I do now."

He turned to J'onn with a wide grin. "Space Dad! Scale of one to ten, how happy are you to see me?"

J'onn gathered Winn in a hug and extended a hand to James. "An immeasurable amount. You *both* are a sight for sore eyes."

"And they have information!" Supergirl announced. She turned toward the portal. "But first, let's turn this off. If Marcus *didn't* catch us, maybe we can use it to get everyone out of here." She glanced around. "Where's Lena?"

"Uh . . . she had something to take care of," said Alex. If her sister knew that one of her best friends had left for a spa day, she'd be crushed.

"I can take care of it," said Winn, trotting over to the arch.

Supergirl pointed out the panel, and Winn pressed a few keys. The arch whined, and the portal disappeared.

"Where are we, by the way?" James glanced around the room at all the alien tech. "I thought everything had reverted to ancient times."

"Everything of this Earth," J'onn corrected. "Which is why Supergirl and I are unaffected, along with the alien artifacts."

Winn raised a hand. "Um . . . if everything of this Earth reverted, then how come James and I . . ." He gestured to his jeans and button-down shirt.

"You arrived after the curse hit," said Alex. "So, luckily, you aren't affected either. Unluckily, you don't speak Latin."

"Neither do you," said James. Alex exchanged an amused look with J'onn and Supergirl. "Do you?"

"We've got some stuff to fill you in on," said Supergirl, gesturing to the door. "For starters, everyone here who isn't alien speaks Latin."

"Consider yourselves lucky that while we're in proximity, I can mentally translate for you," J'onn told Winn and James.

As they walked to the control room, Winn touched everything ancient he saw, from oil lamps to maps to a sling someone had left on a table. After he changed into a DEO toga, Winn ran his fingers over *that* too.

"Did you just discover that you have hands or something?" asked Alex. "Why so touchy-feely?"

"Sorry," Winn said. "I just didn't realize the Rome Dome would be so . . . cool."

"I thought I heard some new voices!" Mon-El entered

the control room. "Winn! James! Glad to see you guys again." He clasped hands with each of them.

Alex crossed her arms. "Mon-El, if you're here, who's watching the prisoners?"

Mon-El's eyes widened. "The prisoners!" Then he smiled. "Just kidding. I asked a couple agents to take my place." He chuckled but trailed off when Alex continued to stare at him. "She doesn't think that's funny, does she?" he said softly to Winn.

"Escaped convict humor isn't for everybody," Winn replied.

Alex, Supergirl, J'onn, and Mon-El told Winn and James what had been happening inside the Rome Dome. Then Winn and James updated them on the outside world.

"People have tried busting through with explosives, diamond-tipped drills, jackhammers," Winn counted off on his fingers. "*Nothing's* worked. And other people are busy freaking out, so with everyone preoccupied, crime has actually gone down a lot."

"Of course, it helps that most of the city is *inside* the dome," James pointed out. "But the cops are hyperaware of what's happening, and the president's even sent in the National Guard."

Supergirl nodded. "That's good to hear. And you said you knew who could help us?"

Winn reached into his messenger bag and pulled out his tablet computer. "There's a guy . . . Jason Blood."

"Don't ask how we know," James chimed in.

Winn flipped his tablet around so the others could see the screen. On it was the image of a man with auburn hair that had a shock of white down its center.

"We've met that guy!" cried Alex.

At the same time, Supergirl said, "That's the guy from the temple."

"We're off to a promising start," said J'onn.

"Jason Blood came to town to give a talk at National City Music Hall," said James. "But according to you guys . . ." He pointed at Supergirl and Alex.

"Marcus built his estate on top of it," said Alex. "So Mr. Blood obviously won't be speaking there."

"But he shouldn't be too hard to find, right?" asked Mon-El. "I mean, how many people are running around this city with skunk-stripe hairdos?"

"Plus, chances are good he'd be staying at a nearby hotel . . . or I guess it'd be transformed into an inn now," said Winn. He placed the tablet on the stone counter in front of him and brought up a digital keyboard. "Let's see what we've got for a signal."

Supergirl tapped his shoulder. "Uh . . . Winn? We're about two thousand years before the Internet."

He tapped her shoulder in return. "Uh . . . Kara? There's sunlight streaming through the Rome Dome."

Supergirl exchanged mystified looks with the others. "So?"

"Sunlight is an electromagnetic wave," said Winn, pressing buttons on his screen. "WiFi, Bluetooth, and satellite data connections are also electromagnetic waves. So if sunlight can penetrate the dome . . ."

"There's a good chance those signals can get through, too." Alex patted Winn on the shoulder. "Freaking genius."

"I knew we kept you around for a reason," said J'onn with a smile.

Supergirl sighed contentedly and leaned against a wall. "Surrounding yourself with smart people really *is* the way to go."

Alex studied her sister. She'd been making a lot of wise-cracks at her own expense lately. They needed to have a chat, sister to sister.

"Just one problem," said Winn, lifting his tablet above his head. "All the stone is making a signal ridiculously hard to find." He glanced at J'onn. "Remember that alien who was running the gambling den with illegal pay-per-view fights?"

"Oh, man," Mon-El interjected, chuckling. "I lost a *lot* of money b—" He paused as all eyes shifted to him. "B. . .

uying Bibles to save the souls of everyone in there." He pressed his hands together piously.

Winn blinked at Mon-El and then shook his head. "Did we confiscate the signal booster from the gambling den?" he asked J'onn.

The DEO director referred to the inventory list Agent Vasquez had handed him earlier. "It appears so. It's in the subbasement."

"Perfect," said Winn, heading in that direction. "I'll be back." He paused. "I totally missed a *Terminator* opportunity, didn't I?"

James chuckled and held up a duffel bag. "I'm gonna change into my Guardian gear. Who knows when the next fight will be."

"I want to hear more about this *Terminator*," said Mon-El, following Winn. "He sounds like a neat guy."

"And *you* are coming with me." Alex tugged on her sister's cape.

"What?" Supergirl stumbled to keep up. "Where?"

"To talk." Alex led her sister to the balcony. When they were alone, she said, "You've been putting yourself down a lot lately. What's up with that?"

Supergirl avoided Alex's gaze. "I don't know what you mean."

Alex tilted her sister's chin so they were eye to eye. "Yes, you do. Don't play dumb, Kara."

"Yeah, well . . . maybe I'm not playing." Supergirl dropped onto a stone bench.

Alex sat beside her. "What do you mean?"

Supergirl stared at her boots. "I'm surrounded by people who are tech geniuses or musical geniuses or directors of government agencies, and I . . . I don't have any of that going for me."

Alex cocked her head. "Have you forgotten that you save the world on a weekly basis?"

"Only because I was lucky enough to land on a planet where the sun gives me superpowers," Supergirl scoffed, and kicked at the ground.

"All right, then. How about the fact that your articles are published in a major magazine?" Alex tried again.

"Lena gets published in magazines, too."

"So?" Alex laughed in disbelief. "Kara, you can both be successful! It's not a competition."

"It kind of feels like it when her list of accolades is long, and mine's . . ." Supergirl pinched her fingers together.

Alex gripped her shoulders. "Kara, listen to me. Nobody's accomplishments diminish *yours*. Yes, Lena's done a lot, but she comes from a different background." Alex put her arm around her sister. "Do you wish you had rich, soulless parents and an evil brother? Because that's what Lena had to put up with to become who she is."

Supergirl shook her head. "Of course not." She wrapped her arms around Alex. "I wouldn't give you up for anything."

Alex squeezed her sister. "And as far as brilliance goes . . . in the last twenty-four hours, you've talked to someone on a different Earth *and* brought two people through a portal. You." She poked Supergirl in the side. "You made those things happen."

Supergirl chuckled and shoved her sister before pulling her close again. "Yeah."

Alex patted Supergirl's leg. "So no more negative self-talk. We've got a city to save."

"Right!" Supergirl jumped to her feet.

Alex glanced down the steps into the control room. "And I've got a Winn Schott to find. He and Mon-El had better not be making a mess of the artifacts room."

Leaving Supergirl to talk with J'onn and James, Alex hurried down the subbasement steps. She could hear a clattering even before she reached the artifacts room. Winn was removing gears from a basket and tossing them aside while

Mon-El ripped open a padlocked metal container. Since Daxam was Krypton's sister planet, he gained powers from Earth's yellow sun, just like Kara did, including superhuman strength.

"Need help?" Alex asked, poking her head through the doorway.

"You'd think with a finite amount of modern tech in here, we'd be able to find the booster." Winn pulled what looked like a solar panel from the basket and frowned at it. "But, yeah, if you're offering, we're looking for a blue box with a light on top . . . like a TARDIS."

Alex grabbed another basket. "I'm assuming that's a nerd reference."

"Af-fir-ma-tive!" Winn said in a robotic voice. He leaned toward Alex and smirked. "That was a Dalek, in case—" Alex gave him a look, and Winn cleared his throat. "You know, Doctor Who went back to Ancient Rome once. Pompeii."

"Doctor Who?" Mon-El shook the contents of his container onto the floor. "Is that a friend of yours?"

Winn sighed and placed a hand over his heart. "If only."

Alex spotted a little blue box. "Is this what we want?" she asked as she extracted it.

"Bingo!" Winn plugged it into his tablet computer and fiddled with the screen. "Aaand we still have a crappy signal, but it's not as bad as before! This should only take a few minutes."

Mon-El peered over his shoulder. "Do you think there's better reception on the roof?"

Winn nodded. "Possibly, but I hate being up that high. I can go out onto the balcony, I guess."

As the trio headed up the subbasement steps, Winn explained what happened to Doctor Who in Pompeii. As they neared ground level, Alex noticed that Winn's words were being punctuated by footsteps from above. Synchronized footsteps.

Alex thrust her arm out to stop Winn and Mon-El. Then she put a finger to her lips, and they all crouched on the steps, listening.

"How did you get in here?" Alex heard J'onn demand.

"Well, that's not a very nice welcome," came a glib reply. "You're not even going to offer me a glass of wine?"

Alex narrowed her eyes. *Marcus,* she mouthed to Mon-El and Winn.

Mon-El clenched his jaw and started to stand, but Alex pulled him back down.

"What are you doing here, Marcus?" Supergirl asked.

Since their voices sounded distant, Alex risked shifting up two more steps. When the control room came into view, she bit back a curse.

Supergirl, James, J'onn, and a handful of DEO agents were facing Marcus and a platoon of Roman soldiers.

Marcus chuckled and strolled closer to Supergirl. Instantly, the DEO agents raised their swords and shields. Marcus's soldiers did the same, but he halted them with a hand.

"It seems I haven't gotten rid of *all* modern technology," he said, stroking his chin. "Yesterday, you contacted another Earth, and just a little while ago, you created a portal."

So much for keeping that *a secret*, Alex thought to herself.

"I did," Supergirl admitted, "but as you can see, I'm still right here."

"Oh, I'm not worried about you leaving, love." Marcus grinned. "Tempus will find you wherever you run. He knows the taste of your soul."

Alex's skin crawled as Marcus's words sunk in.

"Then why are you here?" J'onn asked.

"Because I'm tired of Supergirl meddling in my affairs," said Marcus. He smirked at Supergirl. "Playtime's over. I've come to collect your toys."

"Crap," Alex whispered. "They're coming!" She tugged on Mon-El's sleeve and turned to make sure Winn had heard, but their IT guru was already halfway down the stairs, tablet clutched in one hand. "Mon-El..."

"I'll go tell him," Mon-El said in a low voice, slinking down the stairs.

"The only way you're taking *anything* from this building is over my dead body," Supergirl told Marcus in a lethal voice. The DEO agents raised their swords once more.

"Actually . . ." Marcus snapped his fingers. "It'll be over *hers.*"

His soldiers parted to let one of Marcus's bodyguards through. His arms were covered with fresh bruises and scratches, but over one shoulder he carried his prize: Lena Luthor.

"Lena." Supergirl's face paled, and she hurried forward.

"Ah, ah, ah." Marcus wagged a finger.

Marcus's soldiers stepped in front of the bodyguard, and the bodyguard pressed a dagger point to Lena's side.

"She put up quite a fight." Marcus regarded Lena's unconscious form with amusement. "Took down two of my men and ravaged poor Thrax." He nodded to the bodyguard. "But in the end, she couldn't defeat a vial of sleeping potion."

Supergirl clenched her jaw. "You'd better not have hurt her."

"She isn't hurt," Marcus said without a hint of fear. "Nor will she be if you simply step aside." He made a sweeping motion with one hand.

Supergirl was going to concede; Alex knew it. But that didn't mean she couldn't do something about it.

Alex took the steps down two at a time, catching up with Winn and Mon-El in the artifacts room.

"Winn, tell me you're almost done," she said.

He pointed to the progress bar on his browser. "I need, like, two more minutes."

She nodded and beckoned to Mon-El. "Let's hide whatever alien tech we can before Marcus and his men get here."

Mon-El turned to Winn. "Can I borrow that?" He pointed to Winn's messenger bag while Alex made a beeline for the baskets.

"Um." Alex ran a hand through her hair. "I don't know what to take."

"Anything that has a power switch or looks like it might go *pew-pew-pew!*" Winn said, passing Mon-El his bag.

"Sounds easy enough." Alex dumped a basket onto the floor and sifted through it. She grabbed a black device covered with tiny lights and a rod with a crystal affixed to one end. Mon-El held the messenger bag open as she tossed in the items.

"How's your download coming, Winn?" Alex asked.

He glanced at his tablet. "Two minutes."

"Two minutes!" Alex smacked his arm. "That's what you said two minutes ago!"

"Well, I can't help it!" Winn rubbed his arm. "The reception down here sucks."

Alex ran to the doorway and peeked out just as the first of the soldiers appeared at the base of the stairs.

"You! Stay right there!" the one in front shouted.

Alex smiled indulgently at him before ducking back into the room. "Guys, we have to go. Now!"

But Winn and Mon-El were nowhere to be seen.

"Guys?" She glanced around the room, spotting a crooked mosaic floor tile beneath a table. Blue light from Winn's tablet peeked through a crack, and Alex nudged the floor tile back into place with her foot.

The soldiers entered the room, weapons drawn.

"Who were you talking to?" one of them demanded.

She scratched her head. "Well, I thought my friends were in here, but . . ." She chuckled and shrugged. "I guess they had salutations to get to."

The soldier narrowed his eyes but beckoned to his companions. "We take it all." He pointed his sword at Alex. "And if you interfere . . ."

Alex held her hands up conciliatorily. "Wouldn't dream of it. Please, help yourselves."

The soldiers moved past her, picking up the items Alex had discarded from the basket and clearing the tables of whatever she and Mon-El hadn't been able to grab.

Several of the soldiers gathered around the arch and hoisted it off the floor. Alex watched the soldiers haul away their alien artifacts. None of them seemed aware of Winn and Mon-El beneath the floor tiles.

But then two soldiers grabbed the table above their hiding place.

"Hey, that's not an artifact! That's our furniture," said Alex, hurrying to stop the soldiers.

"We only wish to move it aside," said one of the soldiers, fixing Alex with a look.

She stopped and folded her hands in front of her. "Of course."

The soldiers carrying the transmatter portal shuffled across the room, grunting as they did so.

"Stop, stop," one of the soldiers said. "I need to adjust my grip."

To Alex's horror, the soldiers lowered the arch back onto the floor with one end right on top of Winn and Mon-El's hiding place.

Since they were in a hollow, no crossbeams supported the tile, and as soon as the soldiers shifted the weight from themselves to the floor, the tile cracked and split in two.

Alex couldn't stop the hand that went to her mouth.

The soldier leading the operation stared at her. "What is it?"

Alex shook her head. "Sorry. I was about to sneeze."

She chanced a glimpse at the broken tile and saw it shift as Mon-El momentarily came into view.

He was holding the weight of the broken tile *and* the transmatter portal on his back.

The tile pieces ground together, and Alex flinched, uttering a loud, "A-choo!"

The soldier frowned and stepped back. "Are you ill?"

"I might be." Alex sniffled and nodded. "You should really leave."

"Alex?" Supergirl appeared in the doorway with Marcus, a frown stretched across her face. "Is everything OK in here?"

"Uh . . . yeah," said Alex, forcing a smile. "I'd just really like these soldiers to take the artifacts and go."

Marcus crossed his arms and smirked. "You're eager to part with the portal? That's interesting."

"Hey, you're getting what you want, and we get you out of our hair," said Alex, shrugging. "It's a *win-win* situation, right, Supergirl?" She emphasized the words, hoping her sister would catch the double meaning of Winn's name.

Supergirl cocked her head at Alex, who toed the floor. Supergirl's eyes narrowed one minute and widened the next, and Alex knew she'd spotted Winn and Mon-El with her X-ray vision.

"If you don't want the portal anymore, I can just put it

back." Supergirl quick-stepped to the arch and lifted it off the broken tile.

Alex let out a sigh of relief.

"No, no. We'll still take it." Marcus gestured to his soldiers. "I'll keep it as my personal Arch of Titus, lauding my victory over you." He grinned at Supergirl.

"The week's not over yet," she reminded him.

Marcus's men carried their plundered goods out of the artifacts room while Alex and Supergirl looked on. The portal arch was the last item to be removed.

Marcus wiped his brow, apparently glad to be done with the laborious task of shouting directions. "There now. Was that so difficult?" he asked Alex and Supergirl. "And we've freed up this space so you can use it for whatever you want."

Alex scowled. "Are you actually expecting us to be grateful?"

Marcus blinked. "You're right. I really don't care."

"And what about Lena?" asked Supergirl as Marcus strolled around the room, kicking at scraps.

"I'll have Thrax release her into your custody." He paused beside the broken floor tile, and Alex's whole body tensed. "I just need to grab one last thing."

Marcus crouched and punched through the tile, grabbing Winn by the front of his toga and yanking him from the hollow. "Hello, Winn! Or is it *Winn-Winn*?" Marcus glanced at Alex and smirked.

"Let him go," Mon-El growled, emerging from his hiding place.

"Hey, Marcus." Winn gave a little wave with his free hand, hiding the tablet behind his back with the other. "Cool toga. Is that . . . is that made from local wool or—"

Marcus snatched the tablet from Winn's hand. "I'll take that. And *that*." He yanked Winn's messenger bag off Mon-El's shoulder.

"What do we have in here?" Marcus opened the bag and rifled through the contents. "Could be useful, could be useful. HA-HAAAA!" He extracted Winn's copy of *Demonology for Dummies* and doubled over, laughing.

"It's not *that* funny," Winn muttered.

Marcus wiped at his eyes and thrust the book into Winn's chest. "You keep that, my friend." He hoisted the messenger bag onto his shoulder and turned on the tablet. "Password?"

Winn studied the floor. "One-nine-five-nine."

Marcus tapped in the code and smirked. "'Dear Lyra,'" he read. "'I don't have much time before they catch me, but I wanted you to know how I felt.'"

"You were writing a love note to Lyra while I kept us from being crushed?" Mon-El stared at Winn in disbelief.

Winn shifted from foot to foot. "I'm probably never gonna see her again."

"Definitely not," Marcus agreed, reviewing Winn's browser history. "It's just as well. Your obsession with action figures is alarming."

Winn held up a finger. "They're actually coll—"

Alex elbowed Winn in the side and fixed Marcus with a bitter smile. "You have everything you came for. We'd like you to leave now." She pointed to the doorway.

"Very well." Marcus slid Winn's tablet into the messenger bag. "Stay out of trouble, or I'll kill all your loved ones." He smiled at the group. "Kidding! It'll just be the ones inside the dome. Ta-ta!" He waggled the tips of his fingers at them and swaggered from the room.

Supergirl followed Marcus into the hall while Alex, Mon-El, and Winn stayed behind.

As soon as Supergirl reappeared and flashed a thumbs-up, Alex turned to Winn.

"Tell me you got the info," she pleaded.

Winn scoffed. "Of course!"

"*And* that you erased any trace of your search?" added Supergirl.

Winn brushed dirt from his shoulder. "What am I . . . new?"

Supergirl nodded. "Then I'll clear my calendar for the evening," she said. "For a visit with Jason Blood."

9

I *WONDER IF I SHOULD START CHARGING* *taxi fare*, Supergirl thought as she carried Winn up seven flights of stairs.

Darkness had fallen, and while Alex and Guardian patrolled the streets and Mon-El watched the DEO prisoners, Supergirl, J'onn, and Winn sought out Jason Blood. The demonologist's room was on the inn's fifteenth floor, and Winn's legs had given up on the eighth.

"This is so humiliating," Winn said as Supergirl cradled him in her arms.

"You could've stayed behind with Dr. Hoshi to watch over Lena. *Or* taken the elevator," she reminded Winn with a smirk.

"Elevator?" Winn repeated. "You mean that rickety death box held up with twine?"

Supergirl had to admit it looked precarious, but she'd inspected it with her X-ray vision, and the turnstile-and-pulley system was actually solid. Still, she felt bad for the men having to turn the shaft that raised and lowered the lift.

"Also, these buildings are seriously tripping me out," Winn added. "How are they so much bigger on the inside? They're like . . ." His eyes widened. "They're like TARDISes! And you're Doctor Who!" He pointed to Supergirl and whispered, "Which makes me the doctor's companion. Sweet."

"Uh . . . sure?" Supergirl said. She adjusted her grip on Winn, who flinched.

"Why couldn't we just zip up the outside of the hotel?" he asked.

"That's the exact opposite of covert," said J'onn, his voice reverberating off the walls.

He was flying after Supergirl and Winn in his true form: Martian Manhunter. His green torso was clothed in black body armor that was crisscrossed with a red X.

"We can't risk Marcus finding out where we've gone," added Supergirl.

After one more bend in the stairs, a metal plate appeared on the wall with FLOOR 15 carved into it.

"Here we are." Supergirl lowered Winn to the floor while J'onn transformed back into his Hank Henshaw guise and opened the stairwell door. He peeked down the hallway and beckoned to Supergirl and Winn.

"Say nothing about our business until we're in private once more," J'onn warned them. "We don't know who could be listening."

Supergirl and Winn nodded and followed him toward Jason Blood's room. Halfway to their destination, a door opened to their left. A man and woman emerged and gasped. The woman fell back against the wall, and the man pressed a hand to his heart.

"Supergirl," he whispered.

"Hello," she said with a polite nod.

The woman ran back into her room, and Supergirl reached out after her.

"Wait, please don't be scared!" she called.

But the woman reappeared a moment later holding an apple. She knelt before Supergirl and raised the apple high, bowing her head.

Winn snickered, and J'onn elbowed him.

"Forgive this paltry offering, O Supergirl!" bemoaned the woman.

"Oh! Thank you?" said Supergirl, taking the apple.

The man gave his partner a scornful look. "We can do better."

"No no, that's not necessary!" Supergirl said as the man ran into the room. He trotted back out holding a vase and a golden hourglass.

Mimicking the woman's gesture, he knelt with his offerings above his head.

"Um . . . I'm pretty sure you can't give away the inn's stuff," said Winn.

"My friend is right," said Supergirl. "I can't really—"

The man shook the items at her and pressed them into her stomach. "All hail Supergirl!"

"All hail Supergirl!" the woman chimed in.

"ALL HAIL SUPERGIRL!" the couple said together. "THE GODDESS WALKS AMONG US."

"Oh, boy," said Winn.

Supergirl frowned. This Ancient Roman way of thinking was getting a little annoying.

"Just take the offerings," J'onn whispered to Supergirl. "We can return them later."

She smiled at the man and accepted the vase and hourglass. "I will treasure them always. But now I must go."

The couple beamed at her but didn't move. She couldn't risk them seeing where she, Winn, and J'onn were going, but she also couldn't risk hanging out in the hallway in case other worshipers appeared.

Supergirl puffed out her chest and lifted her chin.

"And . . . um . . . you cannot gaze upon me while I return to Olympus," she said in a deep voice, her eyes narrowed.

"Yes, goddess." The woman tugged the man's arm, and they backed into their room, bowing.

As soon as their door closed, J'onn ushered Supergirl down the hall.

"Quickly. Before someone else appears and offers you their couch."

"What was with the deep voice?" Winn asked as the three of them sprinted down the hall.

"It felt more godlike," Supergirl said with a shrug.

She, Winn, and J'onn stopped in front of Jason Blood's room. Just as J'onn was about to knock, the door opened, revealing the man Supergirl had seen outside the temple.

"Hello," Supergirl said. "Jason Blood?"

Jason looked from her to Winn to J'onn. "I see you've decided to take me up on that chat."

He took the apple, vase, and hourglass from Supergirl.

Then he closed the door in her face.

She blinked at the wooden planks. "What just happened?"

"I don't know." J'onn knocked on the door while glancing at Winn. "This man is supposed to help us with Tempus Fugit?"

Winn chewed on a fingernail. "According to the magical sticky note."

The door flew open, and Jason appeared again, this time with a cloak draped over one arm. His hands were empty save for a key.

"Let's not speak of demons and magic in such quiet spaces." He stepped into the hallway and locked the door to his room. "I prefer a *loud* environment, where we won't be overheard." He pocketed his key and faced the DEO team. "Know any good taverns?"

"There's one on the ground floor," said Supergirl.

Winn groaned. "That's fifteen sets of stairs down! It'll take forever to get there."

"Not if I throw you out the window," offered Jason.

Supergirl stepped between them. "You'll do no such thing!"

Beside her, J'onn hid a smile. "I believe he was joking, Supergirl."

"He was indeed," said Jason. "Lighten up! It's the only way we'll make it out of this alive. Oh, and put this on . . . goddess." He tossed his cloak to Supergirl and strode down the hall. Supergirl glared at his back.

"I saw that," said Jason.

With a sigh, she tied on the cloak and closed it around her uniform.

Jason held the stairwell door open for them. "A human, a Kryptonian, and a Green Martian walk into a stairwell. Sounds like the start of a bad joke," he mused aloud.

All three DEO agents froze.

"You know who I am?" asked J'onn.

"I know your *species*." Jason stepped into the stairwell after them and closed the door. "I don't have the privilege of your name." He scratched his chin. "Yet you all seem to know mine."

J'onn extended his hand. "I am J'onn J'onzz. My friends and I protect this city from . . . unusual threats."

Jason shook it heartily. "Pleasure."

"Winn Schott." Winn offered his hand, as well.

Jason clasped it in his own. "I heard you mention that you got my name from a sticky note. Who gave you the note?"

Winn let out a nervous laugh. "Nobody, actually. It appeared in this demonology book at Nimue's Parlor Tricks."

Jason smiled, and Supergirl could've sworn there was almost a fondness to it.

"Well, well. She still thinks of us after all this time." He chuckled and started down the stairs.

"Old girlfriend?" Supergirl couldn't help asking as she followed him.

"Very old," said Jason. "Ancient."

"That's kind of . . . gross," said Winn.

Supergirl chuckled but stopped when she smelled something fruity. She peered down at Jason.

"Are you eating my apple?"

He shook his head and patted his toga. "Not until later. Say, who's defending the city if you three are with me?"

J'onn told Jason about the DEO and Guardian.

"And how did you get involved in demonology?" J'onn asked in return.

"Necessary survival skill," said Jason. "I faced a lot of evil in my youth and the centuries since."

Supergirl stopped on the stairs of the fifth floor, causing Winn to bump into her and J'onn to bump into him.

"I'm sorry, did you say 'centuries'?" Supergirl asked.

Jason nodded. "About fifteen of them. I'm immortal." He shrugged as if being immortal were as common as being an Aquarius.

The others were quiet for a moment.

"What kind of moisturizer do you use?" Supergirl finally asked.

J'onn sighed.

"What? He's been around for fifteen hundred years,"

she said, shrugging. "If anyone's going to know what works, it's him."

J'onn glanced down at Jason. "How have you survived this long? You can't be human."

"I am on occasion," Jason said with a grin. "But that's a story for another day. We need to get to the tavern."

They resumed their descent in silence for several minutes until Winn asked, "Did you know Nikola Tesla?"

Jason nodded. "We gambled on billiards together."

"You've lived quite a life," said J'onn, opening the stairwell door that led to the lobby.

Ahead of them, they could hear conversation and music from the tavern.

"You don't know the half of it," said Jason, leading the way to a table.

Along the way, a drunken man stepped into their path and thrust a piece of parchment at Jason.

"Games Day in two days! Tell your friends!"

"I don't have any." Jason passed the parchment to J'onn.

"Games Day?" J'onn repeated. "What's the cause for celebration?"

Supergirl knew the cause. It was Marcus's way of gloating about his success over her while disguising it as another bit of Ancient Rome for Valeria.

"Just because!" the drunk man replied. He cheered

and ran off, waving another flyer. Nobody paid him much mind. They were too busy playing dice games and telling rowdy stories.

Supergirl tightened Jason's cloak around her uniform and followed her friends to a corner table. She did her best to ignore all the disapproving stares directed at her from men at other tables. The tavern seemed devoid of women except for servers and some less-than-saintly types.

Once they'd ordered their food and drink, Jason spread his arms and said, "So, tell me what you know."

"A man named Marcus Gaius is behind all this," said Supergirl. "He wanted to resurrect his dead wife and give her the city she missed, so he kidnapped me and another woman named Hannah Nesmith and used us to summon Beelzebub and Tempus Fugit. Beelzebub helped Marcus put his dead wife's soul into Hannah's body, and Tempus helped Marcus turn National City into Ancient Rome. He used my blood and spirit to make it all happen."

Jason rubbed his chin. "The trouble with Tempus is that there's always a time constraint."

Supergirl nodded. "We have until Caesar's Comet leaves Earth's orbit in three days. From what I read in the scrolls, the summoning ritual required certain items. We need to get them back."

Winn nodded. "And from what *I* read, to reverse the curse and banish Tempus, we need to recite the counter-curse flawlessly. That's where you come in." He pointed at Jason.

A server appeared with drinks, and everyone at the table fell quiet until she left.

"You have it almost right," said Jason. "I *will* need to speak the counter-curse and remove the offerings, but to banish Tempus *and* Beelzebub, the altars must be smashed and their remains anointed with special potions I can brew for you."

Supergirl cracked her knuckles. "And I can take care of smashing the altars."

Jason shook his head. "*You* must smash *your* altar, and Hannah must smash hers."

J'onn frowned. "That might be a problem, since some-one else is currently controlling Hannah's body."

Jason shrugged. "If it can't be done, then Hannah's soul will wither away."

Supergirl took a long drink from her goblet and pressed her lips together. "Even if Valeria is in control of Hannah's body, I think I can still reach Hannah." She glanced around at the others. "When I mentioned Hannah's boyfriend, Claude, Valeria disappeared for a second, and Hannah reacted."

"So how do we get Hannah back into total control?" asked Winn.

"This love interest of hers sounds like a good place to start," said Jason. "Perhaps if they see each other, it will be enough for her to overpower Valeria. At least temporarily."

"Then the next question is: How do we find the love interest?" asked J'onn.

Supergirl held up a finger. "When I was interviewing Hannah, she mentioned that she was staying at the Wayward Arms. I bet all the musicians are. We could visit Claude and have him meet Hannah somewhere, then make sure she—I mean Valeria—shows up at the same place."

"But how do you get Valeria to show up?" asked Winn.

Their food arrived then, and this time the silence was due to Supergirl and J'onn devouring what was placed before them.

Jason watched Supergirl and J'onn in fascination. "You'd think they'd never eaten before," he said.

"Oh, Supergirl always eats like that." Winn poked at a fried concoction with tapered ends. "You should see her around pizza and pot stickers."

Supergirl stopped chewing. "There is pizza and pot stickers?"

Jason smirked. "Sorry, no. But there are dough balls and dormice." He pointed at some honey-covered lumps and then at the fried concoction Winn was prodding.

"Dormice? As in rodents?" Winn jerked his hand away. "OK. I'm a vegetarian now."

As much as fried mouse should've disgusted Supergirl, the dishes of olives, grapes, grilled asparagus, and roasted chicken were too delicious to pass up. When Marcus had changed everything into an Ancient Roman setting, the bags of cheese popcorn and the frozen pizzas at her apartment had become bags of corn kernels and . . . nothing.

"You're missing out." Jason grabbed a dormouse by a stump that had once been the tail. "The bones are tiny and soft and—"

"Sooo, how do we get Valeria to meet Claude?" Winn interrupted, looking a little green.

Supergirl popped a grape into her mouth. "They'll have to conveniently run into each other. Although I'm not sure where."

"Humans are creatures of habit," said Jason. "And an Ancient Roman woman with a wealthy husband probably spends every morning helping him pass out food and coins during salutation. Then she'd go to the baths."

"We could have Claude wait for her outside the baths, then," said Supergirl.

Winn nibbled on a piece of bread. "Yeah, that's not at *all* stalker-y."

Supergirl gave him a look. "Do you have a better idea?"

Winn cleared his throat and wiped off his hands. Then he cracked his neck, stalling for effect.

Supergirl rolled her eyes. "Winn!"

"You said you still have the interdimensional extrapolator, right?" he asked.

She nodded. "But Marcus rerouted it to—ohhhh!" She sat up tall and smiled at Winn. "Clever friend!" She raised a hand, and he high-fived it. Then she turned to Jason. "We can totally get Valeria and Claude in touch with each other."

"Good," said Jason. "I'll start making the potions."

Supergirl rubbed her hands together. "We have a plan! I love it. Once we have Hannah back in her body, we break into Marcus's estate, take out all the guards, destroy the altars, sprinkle the potions, and say the counter-curses."

"Yeahhh." Winn narrowed his eyes. "Somehow I have a feeling breaking into Marcus's estate and taking out the guards won't be as easy as you make it sound."

"It could be," said J'onn, holding up the Games Day flyer. "If we do it at the right time."

10

SUPERGIRL AND J'ONN WERE OUTSIDE
Claude's room at the Wayward Arms before sunrise
the next morning. Since people inside the dome
were getting more Roman by the day, Supergirl had a feeling Claude would be leaving soon for morning salutations.

When she knocked on his door, Claude opened it, rubbing his bleary eyes.

"I am still sleeping," he said in a thick French accent.
"Can you come back . . ." His words trailed off as he stared
at Supergirl in awe. "Goddess!"

He dropped to his knees, and Supergirl frowned at J'onn.

"Can you fix this?" she asked. "Get his mind back to
the present?"

J'onn's expression mirrored hers. "Ordinarily, I don't

approve of mental manipulation, but desperate times call for desperate measures," he muttered, closing his eyes.

"Make it quick," said Supergirl as Claude kissed the tips of her boots.

J'onn placed a hand on Claude's head, and a moment later, Claude glanced up at Supergirl and scrambled backward.

"I am so sorry. I don't know why—"

Supergirl raised a hand to silence him. "It's fine. Hannah Nesmith needs your help."

At the mention of Hannah's name, Claude's mouth fell open. "Hannah? My Hannah? You know where she is?" He beckoned Supergirl and J'onn into his room.

"We do," said J'onn. "But you might not believe us."

Claude chuckled nervously and smoothed his hair. "I was just kissing Supergirl's boots, and I am trapped in Ancient Rome. There is little I won't believe at this point."

Supergirl leaned against his dresser. "The same man who did all this"—she gestured around the room—"also kidnapped Hannah. And she's being controlled by . . . um . . . his formerly dead wife."

Claude blinked at Supergirl and J'onn. "You're right. I don't believe you."

Supergirl grunted in exasperation, and J'onn put a hand on Claude's shoulder.

"All you need to believe is that Hannah's in danger. She's not herself, and unless we help her, she never will be again."

Claude rubbed a hand over his face. "What can I do?"

"We were hoping you could come with us and speak to her," said Supergirl. "She might be able to overpower the woman controlling her if she hears your voice."

"Of course!" Claude opened the chest at the end of his bed and pulled out a toga. "Please allow me to change, and I will accompany you."

Claude stepped behind a folding screen to change. His clothing chest still open, Supergirl moved forward and spotted a stringed instrument inside. Its rectangular wooden base had two arms branching out from the top. A bar was affixed between the arms, and from it stretched a series of strings that ran down to the base.

"I guess you don't have your violin anymore, huh?" Supergirl asked.

Claude clucked his tongue in dismay. "It has vanished. In its place, I found the cithara."

"Do you know how to play it?" she asked.

Claude grunted. "It is similar to a guitar, which I can also play, but takes more effort." He emerged from behind the screen. "Lucky for me, I have had nothing else to do here but practice."

"I'm sure you play it just as well as the violin," said Supergirl, at which Claude gave an amused smile.

"You have heard me play violin?"

"Hannah shared a recording with m . . . with a friend of mine," said Supergirl.

Claude smiled wistfully. "Sweet Hannah. Let us go to her. How far away is she?"

"Not far if we fly." Supergirl crossed to the window and opened the shutters.

Claude's eyebrows lifted. "Perhaps I will walk with your friend." He turned to J'onn, who was morphing into Martian Manhunter. Claude swallowed when he saw the completed transformation. "Or . . . maybe by myself."

"You're flying with one of us, so which will it be?" J'onn offered a hand to Claude, who stared at it as if it were a scorpion.

"I think I will go with Supergirl." Claude practically ran to her, and she smiled.

"Try not to scream," she said. "You don't want to wake the neighbors."

Wrapping an arm around Claude, she leaped from the window and flew to the DEO office with J'onn close behind.

When they touched down on the DEO balcony, Claude's hair was as wild as his eyes, but he neither threw up, as Winn had done the first time she took him flying, nor passed out, as James had.

Instead, Claude wobbled down the DEO steps after Supergirl, smoothing his hair.

"Where is Hannah?" he asked.

"That's another unbelievable thing." Supergirl bit her lip. "We can't gain physical access to the place she's being held yet, but we'll be able to communicate with her through an interdimensional extrapolator."

Claude blinked. "Sure," he said.

"This must be Claude." Alex's voice carried over to them, and Supergirl turned toward her sister.

It was all she could do not to burst out laughing.

Alex looked as if she'd dunked her face into a bowl of flour. It was an interesting contrast to her eyebrows, which had been drawn in thick and black. Dark kohl lined her lower lids, and from her upper lids to her eyebrows, the skin was painted green.

"I like the green," commented J'onn, which really did make Supergirl laugh.

Alex stared at the ceiling and sighed. "Maggie wanted to do my makeup, OK? I think the Ancient Roman influence is really getting to her."

Supergirl rubbed at some of Alex's powder. "Well, it's definitely not Maybelline," she said with a snicker.

Alex poked her. "It's not funny. Maggie rubbed dead snails on my face."

Supergirl retracted her hand. "What?"

"We didn't have time to burn them." Alex waved off her explanation. "I don't want to talk about it."

"Well, to answer your earlier question, yes, this *is* Claude," said Supergirl.

After she, Winn, and J'onn had met with Jason the previous night, Supergirl had flown to Alex's apartment to fill her in on the plan.

"And this is Alex Danvers." Supergirl gestured to Alex. "She's not normally so . . . fancy."

Claude nodded to her. "How do you do?" He turned back to Supergirl. "When can I speak with Hannah?"

Supergirl removed the extrapolator from its hiding place in her boot and held it up. "Let's give her a call."

She held down the button, and the window appeared, causing Claude to jump back.

As it had before, the window opened onto Marcus's receiving room, which at the moment was empty. But a flute played softly out of sight, its tune a familiar one.

"Valeria!" Supergirl shouted. "Valeria Messalina!"

The music stopped, and there was a pattering of feet across marble. A moment later, Hannah's face appeared.

"Hannah!" cried Claude.

Hannah stepped closer to the portal and squinted. "You . . . I know you."

"Yes!" Supergirl pushed Claude squarely in front of the window. "This is your boyfriend, Claude."

Hannah blinked and reached out. "Claude."

Supergirl elbowed him. "Talk about your past."

Claude nodded. "Uh . . . when I was a boy, I broke my arm—"

Supergirl elbowed him again. "Your past with *her*! Jog her memory!"

Claude smacked himself on the forehead. "Of course. Hannah, do you remember our trip to Barcelona? The first time you tried the hot chocolate, you thought they'd forgotten the milk."

One corner of Hannah's mouth tilted upward.

"And then we visited the Sagrada Familia and looked at the stained glass," Claude continued. "You said it made you think of living inside a rainbow." He smiled at her.

Hannah smiled back. "That's a nice story."

Supergirl bit her lip. This wasn't going quite like she'd hoped.

"Valeria?" Marcus's voice sounded off in the distance, and Hannah's smile disappeared.

"You must stop visiting me." Hannah's disapproving gaze included Supergirl. "For your own safety."

But safety wasn't Supergirl's concern. She nudged Claude in the back.

"Ask her to meet you somewhere!" she whispered. "For one last good-bye."

Claude pressed his hands together. "Hannah, I will leave you alone . . . *we* will leave you alone"—he gestured to Supergirl—"if you will let me say good-bye in person."

"Valeria?" Marcus pressed. "Where are you, my love?"

Hannah glanced nervously to the side but then nodded. "Very well. Meet me in the temple when the sun reaches its peak. *She* knows the way." Hannah pointed to Supergirl. "Now, please, begone."

"Good idea," said Supergirl, pressing the extrapolator button again.

The window vanished, and Claude dropped to his knees, head in his hands. "What has happened to her?"

Supergirl crouched beside him. "She's under a curse. One we have to break."

"But how?" Claude held open his arms. "Our memories together did not sway her."

"Maybe that's not what she needs," said Supergirl. "There must be something else that can draw her back in."

Before they could ruminate on it any further, Alex tapped Supergirl's shoulder. She'd finally removed her makeup but replaced it with a frown.

"I have something you might want to see."

Supergirl got to her feet and looked at J'onn. "Can you keep Claude company?"

"Of course," said J'onn.

Supergirl followed Alex to the infirmary, where James and Mon-El were leaning against a counter watching Dr. Hoshi dab a brown-tinged ointment under Winn's eye. Winn winced and sucked in his breath through bloodied lips.

"Winn!" Supergirl hurried over. "Are you OK?"

Winn gave her a thumbs-up. "You should see the other guy. He looks . . . better."

Supergirl turned to James and Mon-El. "What happened?"

"We couldn't pay our tab at a restaurant," said Mon-El. "Winn thought he had money, but—"

"I *did*. In a little pouch," Winn said. "Someone must have swiped it." He pointed at Supergirl. "*Don't* tell J'onn."

"You got punched because you couldn't pay for your food?" Alex asked in disbelief.

"No, the punching happened when they tried to explain themselves in Latin." James smirked at Mon-El and Winn.

Supergirl rubbed her forehead. "Mon-El, how many curse words did you use?"

"Me?" Mon-El pointed at himself. "Oh, no, no, no."

"It was me." Winn raised his hand. "I thought I was

apologizing, but according to Mon-El, I called the server a rude name."

Mon-El sucked in his breath and nodded. "A *very* rude name."

"So he punched me," Winn finished.

"OK, I'm going to need you to be quiet for a minute," said Dr. Hoshi. She approached Winn holding a piece of gauze that smelled of alcohol and something else just as harsh. "The astringent I'm about to put on your lip is going to burn like the fires of the underworld."

Winn drew a shaky breath, and Supergirl grabbed one of his hands for support.

"Here we go," said Dr. Hoshi, touching the gauze to Winn's lip.

His eyes opened wide, and he started humming "I Got You, Babe" at the top of his lungs while squeezing Supergirl's hand.

She was equally impressed and pained by how much it hurt.

"Aaand we're done," said Dr. Hoshi, stepping away.

Winn's song trailed off in a whimper, and he lay back on the cot.

"Sonny and Cher?" Alex asked with an amused smile.

Winn nodded, mumbling through the swelling, "My mom used to sing it when I got hurt."

"Awww." Alex put a hand to her heart. "*My* mom sang 'You Are My Sunshine.'"

Supergirl grinned and thought of her own mother, who would sing a Kryptonian folk song to soothe her. It was funny how even across worlds, music could—

Supergirl's eyes widened, and she grabbed Alex's arms. "That's it!"

She darted from the room with Alex calling after her, "Uh . . . glad we could help!"

Claude was standing on the balcony by himself when Supergirl approached him.

"J'onn had to speak with a visitor," he explained. "So I'm waiting and wondering how to reach Hannah."

"Well, wonder no more." Supergirl grinned at him, hands on her hips. "I've got a plan! We just need to swing by your hotel room."

"Before you do, we should discuss an issue that's come up," said J'onn, walking over to them.

"*Another* issue?" Supergirl sighed. "We just got done dealing with Winn's!"

J'onn crossed his arms. "Actually, this concerns Winn. I spoke with the restaurant owner, and the man isn't happy, despite the punches his employee got in."

Supergirl snorted. "What, he wants a second round?"

"No, he wants to see Winn publicly punished," said J'onn without a trace of humor. "In the gladiatorial arena."

11

I F IT HADN'T HURT TO TALK, WINN would've said, "No, no, no. I'd rather fall into a sarlacc pit. No." Instead, he managed a vehement shake of his head when J'onn told him what was coming. Winn had finally been cleared to leave the infirmary and was in the control room with his friends. The last thing he wanted was to be *back* in the infirmary.

"This guy wants to challenge Winn to a gladiator fight?" Alex put a protective hand on Winn's shoulder.

J'onn shook his head. "There's a portion of the games set aside at midday for punishing criminal offenders. Usually, they fight one another, so Winn will face an opponent then. If he doesn't, Marcus's soldiers will find Winn and make a public example of him."

"'Public example'?" The words were out of Winn's mouth before he remembered his split lip, and he winced in pain.

"Tell me they'd only throw tomatoes at him," said Supergirl.

J'onn's expression darkened. "Something far worse, I'm afraid."

Winn wrapped his arms around himself. He missed his Hawaiian daydream.

Supergirl narrowed her eyes. "You know, it's a pretty big coincidence that Winn would get robbed and then be sentenced to a fight hosted by our greatest enemy."

Alex nodded. "I agree. And if Marcus wants to play by his own rules, we can, too." She glanced at J'onn. "You need to shapeshift into Winn tomorrow and fight in his place."

Winn cheered and shook his fists in triumph.

Supergirl touched Alex's arm. "Sorry, but he can't. I need J'onn at Marcus's estate for my plan to work."

Winn groaned and shook his fists in frustration.

"Okay, then *I'll* go in his place," said Mon-El. "Winn and I both have dark hair and dark eyes. From far away, it'll be hard to tell us apart."

Winn cheered again.

"You don't exactly have the same build, Mon-El, and you're at least a foot taller than Winn," Supergirl said. "We just need to make sure we reverse the curse before Winn's midday fight tomorrow."

James cleared his throat and held up a hand. "Don't you think we might be underestimating Winn? I mean, he's survived everything we've been through so far. How did *that* happen?"

Winn mimed running away, and James smacked his arm.

"No, come on, man. I'll bet you've got some moves." He walked to an open space on the control room floor and beckoned to Winn.

Yeah, moves like typing and clicking, Winn thought, but he joined James as his other friends shuffled closer to watch.

"What is happening?" asked the Frenchman who was with Supergirl.

"David's about to take down Goliath." She beamed at Winn.

The Frenchman looked Winn up and down. "He is very short for Goliath."

Winn glowered at him. *I will rip that awesome mustache right off your face.*

James clapped to get Winn's attention and crouched a few yards away.

"OK, I'm unarmed, and I'm about to charge at you," said James. "What do you do?"

Without waiting for an answer, he ran toward Winn, who yelped and twisted to one side. Winn thrust his arms out, protecting his groin behind a raised leg.

J'onn sighed and rubbed his forehead.

"Well, at least he's got quick reflexes," said Mon-El.

"Yeah, that actually went better than I expected," said Supergirl.

What was that supposed to mean?

"You look like a flamingo trying to dab," Alex told Winn. "Put your leg down."

Winn did as she instructed, and Alex stepped beside him. "Don't react until James is within striking distance. And focus on ducking, weaving, blocking, and grabbing."

Alex motioned for James to attack her. He did so, swinging at Alex, who dodged the blow and grabbed the front of James's toga. She pulled him toward her and kicked up both legs, wrapping them around his midsection. Thrown off-balance, James tumbled forward, and Alex used her legs and upper body to flip him over her head and onto his back.

"See?" She rolled to a kneeling position and turned to Winn. "Just like that."

Winn stared at her.

"Yes, watching you do it once is exactly like five years of combat training," he mumbled with a hand to his lip.

"Why don't we start simple," J'onn said, putting a hand on Winn's shoulder.

"While you guys work on that, I'm going to take Claude to see Hannah," said Supergirl. She paused next to Alex and whispered something.

"Hey, no secrets," Winn mumbled again. But no one paid his comment any attention.

Supergirl backed away and waved to the others, then took off into the air with the Frenchman.

Alex nudged Winn. "Come on. We're going to teach you how to slip a punch."

Winn groaned, but he partnered up with Mon-El while Alex and James faced each other.

165

"The important thing to remember," said James, "is that people can only punch as far as they can reach." He raised his arms and threw a slow-motion punch at Alex. "So if you move out of range, you won't get hit."

Alex slipped to one side, avoiding James's fist. She gestured for Winn and Mon-El to try.

Winn arched an eyebrow at the Daxamite prince and pointed at his injured lip. The last thing he wanted was wounds on top of wounds.

"I'll be gentle," Mon-El promised, raising his fists.

Winn raised his, too, and Mon-El feigned a punch. Instantly, Winn jerked his head aside.

"Better," said Alex. "Try to grab Mon-El's arm as it slips past. Then he'll have to reach across to strike you with his other hand."

Mon-El repeated the gesture, and Winn grabbed him. Mon-El swung again, and Winn ducked.

"That's it!" said Alex while J'onn clapped.

"Trust your instincts," J'onn added.

"Now let's work on deflecting punches." James gestured to Winn. "Try to hit Mon-El."

Winn clenched his fists and jabbed. Mon-El pushed the strike aside with his hand. Winn took another swing, and Mon-El knocked it aside again.

"Now, Winn, switch roles with Mon-El and let him try and hit you," said James.

"Wait, wait, wait." J'onn grabbed James's Guardian helmet off a table. "If you'll permit me, I'm getting a little uneasy." He offered the helmet to Winn.

Winn put it on and nodded at Mon-El. After successfully knocking aside nine punches, Winn mumbled, "Time- out."

But just as he lowered his arms to catch his breath, Mon-El threw punch number ten.

It was a light punch by superhero standards, but Winn still flew across the room, crashing into an oil lamp and sprawling on his back. There was a chorus of "Oooh!" followed by a rush of footsteps.

"Owww." Winn gazed up at the ceiling through the helmet's eye slits.

"Winn!" James's concerned face came into his field of view. "You OK?"

Mon-El loomed above him, too. "Sorry, man. I thought you were gonna parry."

Alex helped Winn remove the helmet, and he scowled at Mon-El.

"I said 'time-out.' I needed a break."

J'onn towered over Winn, Alex, Mon-El, and James. "If he gets winded just blocking punches, he's nowhere near ready for a fight."

This time, James didn't argue. "Yeah, you're right," he said.

J'onn glanced at Alex for her agreement, but Alex was studying Guardian's helmet.

"Agent Danvers?" J'onn prompted. "What do you think?"

She grinned up at him. "I think we should visit a blacksmith. Winn needs some armor."

Supergirl was truly grateful for Claude's help, but his nervous pacing was starting to drive her crazy. They were standing next to a food stall near the temple, waiting for Hannah to arrive.

"What if she doesn't show?" asked Claude.

"She'll show," Supergirl assured him, adjusting the cloak she wore so it fully hid her costume. "Deep down, she knows she's meant to be with you."

Claude smiled. "Really?"

Supergirl nodded. *At the very least, she'll do it to get rid of us*, she told herself.

Claude stopped pacing, and his face lit up. "There she is!"

Supergirl grabbed his arm to keep him from sprinting toward Hannah.

"She's surrounded by guards. Let's not make a scene." Supergirl raised the hood of her cloak. "We're just two regular people going to have our livers read."

She and Claude entered the temple, heads bowed, acting oblivious to Hannah's presence. Once inside, Supergirl lowered her hood and squinted against the dim lighting.

"OK, it looks fairly empty, and I don't see any of Marcus's goons," she whispered.

She led the way to a shadowed bench, where she and Claude sat and awaited Hannah's arrival. Claude reached into a satchel he'd brought and removed a cloth-covered bundle.

The temple doors opened, and Hannah argued with one of her guards before entering the building alone. Supergirl turned to give Claude the OK, but he'd already unwrapped his cithara and balanced it on his knees.

Claude strummed the first chord, and everyone in the temple glanced at him. Hannah tilted her head to one side. Claude strummed a few more chords, and the other parishioners resumed their business. But Hannah stepped closer.

Claude delved into the full song, fingers moving deftly along the strings as if he'd played a cithara his whole life. Supergirl closed her eyes and remembered the first time she'd heard the song . . . how the violin had moved her to tears. The song was just as powerful now.

A lump built in Supergirl's throat, and when she opened her eyes, she saw Hannah crying. The woman pressed a hand to her heart, blinked once, twice, and then her expression changed from uncertainty to unbridled joy.

"Claude!" Hannah rushed forward, arms outstretched.

"Hannah!" he cried.

"I'll take that." Supergirl reached for Claude's cithara so he could get to his feet.

He embraced Hannah and gave her a long kiss. Several people looked on with disdain, but Supergirl rolled her eyes.

"Oh, don't judge," she said. "Some of you are probably here to pray for love like this."

Claude and Hannah finally separated and gazed at each other.

"Is it really you?" asked Claude. "Or the other woman?"

Hannah's expression grew troubled, but she nodded. "It's me, but she's still with me. I can feel her trying to take over."

"Well, you need to fight for control." Supergirl approached Hannah and Claude. "At least until you destroy your altar."

Claude glanced from one woman to the other. "Hannah, my love, this is Supergirl. She's the one who brought

me to you."

"It's lovely to meet you, Supergirl." Hannah reached for Supergirl's hand, smiling, but it quickly turned into a frown. "Wait a minute. Did you say something about an altar?"

With a quick glance at the temple doors, Supergirl filled Hannah in. The longer she spoke, the more pale the composer's face became.

"So unless you want Marcus's dead wife to have your body, you must stay in control," Supergirl finished.

"Oh, you don't have to worry about that," said Hannah, rubbing at the goose bumps that had risen on her arms. "Now that I know, she won't stand a chance."

Supergirl nodded. "You'll also need to give Marcus a

reason that you're staying home tomorrow and not attending the games. I'm sure he'll expect you to be there."

Both Hannah and Claude gaped at her in horror.

"You want me to go back to that monster?" asked Hannah.

"I won't allow it." Claude hugged her close.

"I wish it could be different," said Supergirl. "But he'll get suspicious if you stay the night somewhere else."

Hannah didn't argue, but she didn't look pleased, either. "What if he tries to kiss me?"

"Tell him you aren't feeling well," said Supergirl. She snapped her fingers. "That can be your excuse for missing the games!"

Hannah took a deep calming breath, then nodded. "All right."

"An hour or so after Marcus leaves, my friends and I will come to your front door," said Supergirl. "The guards may try to turn us away, but you have to let us in."

Hannah rubbed her neck but nodded again. "Anything else?"

Supergirl pressed her lips together. If the altars had to be destroyed before Jason could pour his potions and speak his counter-curses, Supergirl needed to find out if the altars were somewhere on the estate. She hated to ask more of Hannah, though. The poor woman was a musician, not a fighter.

"Just . . . stay safe tonight," said Supergirl as Claude kissed Hannah's forehead. "And as much as I hate to tear you two apart, Marcus's guards are bound to check on you soon. You should leave us."

Hannah shook her head. "I instructed them to wait outside."

Claude squeezed her hand. "Supergirl is right. We cannot risk them catching us together."

Hannah's lower lip trembled, and she threw her arms around Claude. She gave him a parting kiss and walked to the front of the temple. Claude's eyebrows furrowed, and his nostrils flared, but he turned his back on Hannah and wrapped his cithara in its blanket.

"So." Supergirl rubbed her hands together. "I'm pretty sure Hannah won't let Valeria take over again, but if she does—"

"I'll be waiting and watching," said Claude. "Just tell me where Marcus lives."

Supergirl gave him the directions to Marcus's estate. "After Hannah's altar is destroyed, get her out of there as quickly as possible and go into hiding. Marcus will be looking for her."

Claude pressed his lips together and nodded.

Supergirl bumped his shoulder and smiled. "Hey, lighten up. It's the only way we'll make it out of this alive."

Claude smirked and tucked his cithara under one arm. "When shall I meet you tomorrow?"

"Just after sunrise, once Marcus and his guards have left for the coliseum. Until then, keep a low profile, and if you need me, I'll be at DEO headquarters."

Supergirl moved toward the exit. Knowing that Marcus's guards would be right outside, she slouched, pulled her hair into a ponytail, and put on her glasses and stola, assuming her Kara Danvers identity.

The guards didn't give her a second glance.

As soon as she'd walked a city block, someone fell into step beside her.

"Hello, Supergirl."

Kara step-stuttered but kept walking. "Hello, Jason." She glanced at the demonologist out of the corner of her eye. "How'd you know it was me?"

"The same way I know J'onn J'onzz is a Green Martian," said Jason. "Your souls speak to me. Plus, those glasses are a terrible disguise."

"They fool everyone else in this city," Kara informed him. Then his previous words registered. "And my soul *speaks* to you? I didn't give it permission." She wrapped her cloak more tightly around herself as if it might shield her soul from exposure.

Jason cracked a smile. "When you deal with demons for centuries, you pick up a few tricks along the way," he said cryptically. "How did things go with Hannah?"

"She's back to her old self," said Kara. "How's the potion-making going?"

"I have almost all the ingredients I need," said Jason. He was jogging now to keep up with her. "Where are you off to with such deliberate intent?"

"I need to find out how many guards are at Marcus's estate."

"Twelve," said Jason, not breaking stride. "Six inside, six out."

Kara raised an eyebrow. "Let me guess. You spoke with their souls?"

"I snuck onto the estate to retrieve some of Hannah's blood for a potion."

Kara stopped in her tracks and gawked at him. "You can't do that!" She lowered her voice when she realized other people were staring. "If Marcus saw you—"

"Nobody saw me," he said. "I snuck in when it was dark."

"How?" Kara crossed her arms.

"Teleportation."

Kara squinted at Jason. "Do I want to know—"

"No."

Kara sighed. "Well, even though I don't support you sneaking in alone, did you locate the altars?"

"I did," said Jason.

"Really?" Kara smiled. "Let's go back to DEO headquarters and map it out."

Jason nodded. "We will. First, I need you to complete the banishing potion." He pointed to a side street. "This way."

"You want me to make a potion?" asked Kara. "Sorry, but I failed that class at Hogwarts." She snort-laughed, stifling it when Jason didn't crack a smile. "That would've gone over so much better if Winn were here."

"Sure," said Jason. "But you misunderstand. I don't need your help making the potion. I literally need you *for* the potion. The ritual to banish Tempus Fugit requires the same ingredients as the summoning: your blood and your breath."

Kara wrinkled her nose. "Great. Lead the way."

They took the side street to a shop with boarded-up windows. Its front room was simply decorated with a couch and table, but Jason led Kara through a curtain at the back. Instantly, Kara felt heat wash over her from a fire blazing in a corner hearth. A kettle of bubbling liquid hung above it.

"This should only take a few moments," said Jason. "I just have to sterilize my dagger."

He unsheathed the blade from a holster at his waist and approached the fire.

Kara frowned. "Um, I hate to spoil your plans to stab me, but I have impervious skin. That's not gonna work."

"You might be impervious to most things," agreed Jason. He ran the blade over the flame. "But not Kryptonite, and not this. I've had it for centuries, and there's nothing it can't cut."

Kara snorted. "Yeah, well, we'll see about that."

"Hold out your hand, palm up, please." Jason grabbed a small bottle from the kitchen table and held it beneath Kara's outstretched hand. With an apologetic smile, he said, "This may hurt a bit."

"I highly d—OWWW!"

Jason only punctured Kara's palm with the point of the dagger, but it felt as if he'd ripped the skin from her hand.

"The pain is fleeting," he promised, collecting her blood drops in the bottle. "And by the way, since the dagger worked, it means you're vulnerable to magic."

He handed Kara a piece of gauze to put over the puncture wound.

"That blade is made of magic?" she asked, pressing the gauze to her palm. The pain was already subsiding.

"*Some* magic," said Jason. "Along with iron and steel. I found it during the Crusades."

He brought the blood-filled bottle to Kara's lips.

"Oh, I am *not* drinking that," she said, backing away. "Once something leaves my body, I don't want it back."

Jason rolled his eyes. "I need you to breathe into the bottle. The spirit of a champion?"

Kara laughed sheepishly. She felt less and less like a champion these days. "Right. Of course."

She blew into the bottle, and as soon as her breath fogged the glass, Jason wedged a piece of cork into the vessel and swirled the contents around.

"Will you need Hannah's breath, too?" Kara asked.

Jason shook his head. "Her ritual was for a soul displacement, which is different than a time displacement like yours. Her blood alone will suffice." He eyed Kara's bandaged hand.

"I must say, I'm impressed that someone so young would risk her life to help others. Most people wouldn't."

Kara smirked. "I think you underestimate people. They care quite a bit. I mean, why do *you* do this?"

Jason chuckled. "In the beginning, I did it for selfish reasons—in hopes of saving my soul. Now I do it in hopes of making a better world to live in." He scoffed. "So I guess I'm still doing it for selfish reasons."

Jason poured the blood-and-breath mixture into the kettle, and a cloud of yellow smoke billowed upward.

Kara shook her head. "I can't imagine being immortal, outliving everyone I know. Does losing people ever get easier?"

"For me, yes." He stirred the contents of the kettle and removed it from the heat. "For you, I hope it never does."

Kara blinked and frowned. "*That's* a little mean."

Jason shook his head. "If it gets easier, it means you've lost compassion." He fixed his eyes on hers. "And if *you* lose compassion, Supergirl, then the world is lost."

She nodded slowly. "I won't let that happen. Ever."

"Good," said Jason, funneling the potion into another bottle. "Then we're in good hands."

Kara smirked. "If we can reverse the curse."

He nodded and hid the potion in an urn. "In that case, we'd better get to the DEO. We've got everything we need now . . . except a plan of attack."

12

KARA NEVER THOUGHT SOMEONE brave enough to deal with demons would be such a chicken when it came to flying. But by the time she touched down with Jason on the DEO balcony, her side ached from where he'd dug his fingers into her flesh, and as soon as his feet were on solid ground, he leaned over the balcony and threw up.

Kara wrinkled her nose and patted him on the back. "I'm going to change my clothes. You . . . keep doing what you're doing."

She zipped into a storage room and reemerged as Supergirl. When she returned to the balcony, she saw Jason now sitting on the steps.

"For someone who's been around for centuries, you'd think you would've flown once or twice," she said, offering him a hand.

"In airplanes, yes." Jason let Supergirl hoist him to his feet. "But not in the open air, and *never* upside down."

"I thought you'd enjoy it!" she said with an apologetic shrug. "My sister always does." She glanced around. "Speaking of which, where is she?"

Supergirl entered the control room, where Agent Vasquez was poring over a scroll. "Agent Vasquez, have you seen my sister?"

Vasquez nodded and pointed down the hall. "She and some of the others just got back from buying armor for Winn. I think they're testing it now."

Supergirl scowled and narrowed her eyes. "They're what?"

Not waiting for a reply, she stormed down the hallway with Jason hurrying after her.

"Why are we upset?" he asked.

Supergirl skidded to a stop.

"*That's* why." She pointed at the viewing window of a sparring room. "They're turning our IT guy into a gladiator!"

A figure clad in leg guards, a breastplate, arm wraps, and shoulder guards stood next to Mon-El and James, speaking through a visored helmet. Mon-El reached up to adjust the visor, but when he saw Supergirl, he froze.

The ultimate sign of guilt.

Supergirl pushed the door open and entered the room.

"Hey, babe," said Mon-El with a nervous smile. "You're back sooner than we thought."

"What is this?" She gestured at the armor.

"Arena gear," said James, presenting it with a flourish. "Looks pretty good, right?"

"Absolutely not." Supergirl slashed the air with one hand. "I *told* Alex not to let Winn fight. Under any circumstances."

"I wasn't planning on it," said Winn.

Except his voice wasn't coming from beneath the visor.

It was coming from behind Supergirl.

She whirled around and saw Winn leaning against the doorframe.

"How—?" She turned back to the armored figure. "Who—?"

Before she could use X-ray vision on the visor, the wearer lifted it and smiled at Supergirl.

"Hey, sis," said Alex. "Like my arena gear?"

Supergirl's mouth fell open, but when she looked from Winn to Alex, it slowly closed, and she beamed at her sister.

"Have I ever told you how awesome you are?" She raised her right hand for a high five.

"Wait a minute." Jason stepped forward as Supergirl and Alex slapped palms. "She's going into the arena in place of him?" He pointed to Winn.

Alex raised an eyebrow. "You got a problem with that?"

Jason shrugged. "Can you even fight?" he asked Alex.

Supergirl chuckled and rested a hand on her sister's shoulder. "Oh, if you keep questioning her, you'll find out."

"She's really good," said Mon-El.

"She's beaten me in arm wrestling," confessed James.

Jason didn't look convinced. "And you don't think anyone will notice the difference between Winn and Alex?"

Alex scoffed. "My own *sister* didn't know it was me. Plus, Winn and I have the same body structure."

"Ugh. Don't remind me." Winn tried to push one of his biceps into place. "I *so* need to join a gym."

"There's a gym here," Mon-El informed him.

Winn hesitated. "Yeah, but all the equipment is ancient. Like, literally." He gestured around them.

Jason cleared his throat. "Marcus is already suspicious of you. Won't he think to make sure it's Winn under the visor?"

"That's why Winn will be wearing a set of armor, too," said Alex. "I'll walk in with him, wearing a cloak over my armor, and when it's his turn to fight, we'll switch places."

"Plus, it'll make Marcus *less* likely to think we're up to something if he sees Alex on the sidelines." J'onn entered the room. "Especially since Supergirl will be with her."

Supergirl opened her mouth to protest, but J'onn stepped out of the doorway to reveal a woman cloaked from head to toe. Her face was hidden by the hood, but blond tendrils peeked out from beneath it.

Supergirl frowned. "We don't have any blond, female DEO agents."

She reached for the woman's hood and pushed it back. The blond curls fell back, as well, revealing Dr. Hoshi's ebony hair.

"They told me blondes have more fun, but I refuse to believe it," said the doctor.

Supergirl laughed. "Wow. You guys took care of everything."

"Everything involving the arena," J'onn clarified. "Were you able to get through to Hannah?"

"Claude was," said Supergirl. "She's agreed to skip the games and destroy her altar."

J'onn nodded. "And what about the potions?"

"Cooling as we speak," said Jason. "Now we need to discuss how to get into Marcus's estate."

"Easy," said Supergirl. "We go through the front door."

Jason did a double take. "How's that?"

"J'onn will pose as Marcus, bringing me back to his estate, and you, Claude, James, and Mon-El will pose as the guards escorting me," Supergirl said.

"I finally get to help?" Mon-El perked up.

"*If* you agree to stick to the plan and not go on a vendetta against Marcus," said Supergirl. "There are millions of lives at stake, including mine."

Mon-El crossed his heart. "I promise."

I won't do anything to jeopardize this, was the true meaning Supergirl heard. She smiled in satisfaction.

"Not to poke holes in your plan, but don't the guards all know each other?" Alex asked Supergirl.

"We'll say our guys were spies that nobody knew about," said Supergirl with a shrug. "The guards aren't going to question their boss."

"Hmm." Jason rubbed his chin. "It's rudimentary, but . . . I like it."

"After that, we meet up with Hannah, destroy the altars, and banish the demons." Supergirl brushed her hands together. "National City will be back to normal by lunchtime."

"If everything goes off without a hitch," Alex said with a smirk. "Which never happens."

"But we always find a way to make things work," Supergirl reminded her.

J'onn put a hand on her shoulder. "Yes, we do. Now, if you'll excuse me, Dr. Hoshi and I have a project that needs our attention. Doctor?"

The doctor nodded and followed him from the room.

Alex rotated her arms and twisted from side to side. "I need to break in this armor. Want to spar?"

James grinned. "Who are you talking to? Me, Jason, Mon-El, or Supergirl?"

Alex stretched one of her legs. "All of you."

Supergirl laughed. "OK, but let's not go too hard. You still have a fight tomorrow."

Winn nudged Supergirl. "Actually, can I talk to you for a second? Alone?"

"Sure." Supergirl left the sparring room with Winn.

"Come at me, boys!" she heard Alex shout at her other friends.

"What's up, Winn? Oh! I made a Hogwarts reference earlier today," Supergirl said, bouncing on her toes.

"That's great, Kara," Winn said with half a smile. "Um . . . did you really tell Alex not to let me fight?"

Supergirl stopped bouncing. "Well, yeah." She laughed. "You aren't exactly—"

"And earlier, when James charged at me, and I panicked, you said that was better than you expected." Winn crossed his arms.

Supergirl held up a finger. "Yes, but I also compared you to David from David and Goliath."

"Right. The scrawny guy who could only beat someone with help from God." Winn pressed his lips together.

Heat began to rise in Supergirl's cheeks. "That's not how I meant it."

Winn studied the floor. "Kara, you're one of my best friends, and it would be nice if you believed in me."

"Winn." Supergirl grabbed one of his hands. "Of course I believe in you."

"You don't believe I'm strong enough to win a fight."

"Not without proper training, no," Supergirl admitted. "But you don't have to be physically strong. You're mentally strong! Why do you think I jumped through a portal to bring you here?" She squeezed his hand. "We need your brilliance."

Winn pulled his hand away. "That's another thing. *You* brought *me* here. I should've been the one to do that."

Supergirl shook her head. "It doesn't matter who did it. It's not . . . a competition."

She stepped back and blinked. Alex had had this conversation with *her* just the other day. Winn might not have the exact same insecurities, but he had moments when he felt less than impressive, too.

Then Supergirl thought about how hard James tried to be a superhero. And how excited Mon-El was to finally be going on a mission instead of stuck as a guard. And how Alex used to think she couldn't quite live up to what Kara was. And how Dr. Hoshi thought of herself as a plain old doctor.

Everyone had a reason to feel less than good enough.

But that didn't make it true.

"Winn Schott, you are amazing," she said in a firm voice. "In a way that only you can be. Just like James is amazing in his own way, just like Alex is, just like Mon-El is—"

"And just like you are," said Winn.

This time, Supergirl didn't brush off the compliment.

"Yes. And Kara Danvers, too." She smiled. "And you're strong enough to beat *any* opponent. But in your own way." She tapped the side of her head. "And it isn't physical combat."

Winn grinned and ducked his head. "Yeah, OK."

Supergirl pointed to the sparring room. "Although, if you want to join us . . ."

Winn's eyebrows shot up. "You know what? I'd love to, but I'm . . . uh . . . gonna go reflect on our conversation." He backed away. "Plus, I wouldn't want to put you guys to shame."

"That's very thoughtful," Supergirl said.

Winn walked off, and Supergirl opened the door to the sparring room. James was wiping sweat off his forehead, Mon-El was crouching to pounce, and Jason and Alex were kicking, punching, and doing aerial maneuvers off the walls.

Supergirl grinned and jumped into the fray.

She might as well have a little fun before morning.

Apart from toilet paper, sneakers, and deodorant, the thing

Alex missed most from modern times was coffee. Especially when she was getting up before the sun.

The best she could do for a wake-up jolt was a glass of cold water over her head.

"Are you sure you want to fight in the arena?" Maggie squinted at her from the edge of the bed and yawned. "You guys can just storm Marcus's estate and skip it."

Alex yawned, too, shaking her head. "We don't want to give him any reason to be suspicious. If he sees me and 'Supergirl' there," she said, making air quotes, "it'll buy the real Supergirl some time."

Maggie nodded. "Well, at least let me help with your makeup." She started to get up, but Alex pushed her back down.

"Uh . . . you know, I think I'm gonna skip the makeup today. In case I sweat, because . . . ugh." Alex made a gesture of makeup running into her eyes.

"Smart thinking," said Maggie. "Well, what time is the fight? I'll be sure to be there."

"J'onn said the fights start at noon," said Alex, "but there's a parade at sunrise that Winn has to appear at, and then he'll be sequestered until his—*my*—fight."

Maggie frowned. "Just be careful."

Alex scoffed. "I took down two big guys yesterday. One will be a breeze."

There was a knock at the front door, and Alex hurried to get it. When she opened it, Dr. Hoshi and Winn were on the other side, but instead of returning her smile, they looked panicked.

"What is it?" Alex asked. "What's wrong?"

Dr. Hoshi jerked her head toward Winn. "Ask him."

Alex turned her attention to Winn. "What's with the sad face?"

"Se cont spuall dat in," he replied.

Alex shook her head. "What?"

"From and till," Winn said with a nod.

"He wasn't affected by the curse," explained Dr. Hoshi.

Alex closed her eyes and sighed. "So, he doesn't speak Latin."

"And we don't speak English," added Dr. Hoshi. "And J'onn isn't here to link us."

Alex gave Winn a thumbs-down. He nodded and drew a finger across his throat.

"No." Alex shook her head. "It'll be OK." She made an *OK* gesture with her fingers. "We'll just have to use charades."

The word "charades" must have sounded the same in both languages, because Winn made a face and pointed at Alex while grabbing his nose.

"I do not stink at charades!" she said, even though it was technically true. "Let's just go."

Alex pulled a cloak over her armor and pinned it shut so only her boots showed. She kissed Maggie good-bye, earning another "Be careful," and motioned for Dr. Hoshi and Winn to follow her down the stairs. The closer they got to the ground floor, the louder the sounds of the street became: excited voices and hurried footsteps as people headed to the games and joined the procession into the coliseum.

Soon Alex heard a trumpet blast and a cheer from people on the street below.

"I think the procession's starting," said Alex.

She, Winn, and Dr. Hoshi paused at a stairwell window.

City Hall was a madhouse of floats, caged and chained wild animals, musicians, acrobats, and other performers. And before them all stood a man in a horse-drawn chariot. Alex only needed one guess to figure out who it was.

"Marcus," she said.

With a crack from Marcus's whip, the horses surged forward, and the motley crew of procession attendees fell into line behind their leader.

Alex nudged Dr. Hoshi and Winn, and they continued down the stairs.

The walk to the arena wasn't long, and as they approached the entry gates, Alex reached for Winn's arm, pushing to the front of the crowd that watched the procession.

"Let's wait right here," she told Dr. Hoshi. "I want Marcus to see us."

Dr. Hoshi nodded and pulled her hood up so only the blond hair showed. Alex helped Winn put his helmet back on and lifted the visor so Marcus would be sure to see Winn's face and know he'd shown up.

Alex heard the trumpet blasts again and the thunder of hundreds of feet as the procession approached. At the sight of Marcus, Alex stiffened, but he was busy smiling and waving at the crowd, occasionally tossing out a small bag of coins or food.

As the chariot rolled past, Alex cupped her hands around her mouth and booed. Dr. Hoshi kept her head down but did the same.

Marcus scowled and scanned the crowd for the dissenters. When his eyes fell on the DEO agents, his frown turned into a broad smile. He waved and tossed a bag of what looked like birdseed to Alex before urging his horses into the coliseum.

"Ooh!" She reeled back her arm to throw the bag back, but Dr. Hoshi took it from her. "We wanted attention but not too much attention, right?"

Alex lowered her arm and adjusted the satchel that held her helmet. They watched the procession follow Marcus into the coliseum, and when it tapered off, Alex turned to Dr. Hoshi.

"After I defeat my opponent, meet me under the coliseum, and we'll all leave together."

The doctor nodded. "I'll be sitting as close to ground level as possible. Look for me if you need me."

"Hopefully, it won't come to that." She smiled at the doctor and squeezed her shoulder. "See you, 'Supergirl.'"

Alex hooked her arm through Winn's, and they joined the end of the procession. They entered the massive ring in a cloud of dust and kicked-up sand, marching behind some jugglers to the cheers and jeers of the audience. Once the procession had made one lap inside the coliseum, the members were directed by guards down various ramps to the underground area.

"What are you here for?" one of them asked Winn.

"He's here for the midday fights," said Alex, resting a hand on Winn's shoulder.

"Let a man speak for himself, woman." The guard continued to stare at Winn. "Well?"

Alex growled in frustration. "He's mute, so he can't answer you." She stepped directly in front of the guard. "You'll have. To talk. To me."

The guard sighed and consulted a scroll. "His name?"

"Winn Schott."

For some reason, the guard laughed as he pointed toward a ramp. "You and your *fighter* can wait down there."

"Thank you," said Alex, giving the guard a backward glance as she and Winn walked away. Something about the way he'd said the word "fighter" felt off.

The ramp descended into darkness. Halfway down, Alex glanced around to make sure nobody was close by and nudged Winn.

"Time to switch places," she said, pulling her helmet from her knapsack.

Winn removed his helmet, breathing a deep sigh. He said something unintelligible and laughed.

"I'm betting that was a nerdy joke about Russell Crowe in *Gladiator*," she said, donning her helmet.

"Russell Crowe?" Winn puffed out his chest and smiled.

Alex rolled her eyes. "I wasn't saying . . . oh, never mind."

Winn tossed his helmet into her knapsack and helped Alex fasten *her* helmet straps, still chatting in English.

"Yeah, yeah, hurry up before someone sees," she said, fumbling with the pins of her cloak. She removed it and tied it around Winn's shoulders before lowering her visor.

Winn threw back his shoulders and strolled with authority down the ramp. Alex was right beside him, doing her best impersonation of Winn. He watched her for a moment and frowned.

"What? That's how you walk," said Alex.

Another guard was waiting in the corridor at the bottom of the ramp, and before he could pose a question, Winn pointed to Alex.

"Winn Schott," he said.

The guard consulted a piece of parchment hanging on the wall and clucked his tongue.

"Hold out your hands," he told Alex. "Weapons check."

Weapons check? she thought, doing as he directed. *Of course I have a weapon. How else—*

The guard clapped a set of cuffs around her wrists.

"Whoa!" Winn reached out to stop him, but the guard elbowed him aside.

"What—" Alex started to say but stopped herself when she realized she was supposed to be imitating a man. She coughed instead and shook her cuffed wrists at the guard.

"There's been a change in the program," he informed her before taking her sword and tossing it onto a pile of other weapons.

The guard pushed Alex toward a group of citizens, twenty in total. Some were wearing armor like hers, but most were in tunics or togas. Alex heard the clinking of metal and saw that they were all cuffed and linked to one long chain.

"This is the last of them!" The guard called up the line as he ran a section of chain through Alex's cuffs.

Someone toward the front tugged on the central chain, and everyone attached to it lurched forward.

Alex glanced back at Winn, who had a panic-stricken look in his eyes.

"Al . . .Winn!" he called, extending a hand to her.

Alex shook her head and twisted her body so he could see her hands. Then she flashed him two thumbs-up.

There was another tug on the line, and Alex stumbled forward, following the group up a ramp and into the coliseum. As soon as the first person on the chain stepped into sunlight, the crowd went wild. They quickly fell silent, however, and fixed their attention on the north end of the coliseum. Alex followed their eyes to a fancy viewing box where Marcus stood with hands raised to quiet the crowd.

"Good morning, and thank you all for celebrating these glorious games with me!" he shouted.

He lowered his hands to allow for uproarious applause and then raised them again.

"My dear wife, Valeria, has taken ill and won't be attending." Marcus paused for sympathetic sounds from the crowd. "In her delirium, she has asked that I not harm any of the beasts you see here today." He gestured to the ring, and cages containing half a dozen lions appeared.

There were gasps and shouts of fear from the people

chained to Alex, but they were quickly drowned out by a guttural roar from one of the lions.

"I will honor my beloved's wishes and more!" he announced. "Not only will I not harm the animals, but I will *feed* them . . . the criminals in this ring!"

The audience broke into wild applause and cheers, and Alex's heart dropped into her boots.

Marcus said something she couldn't hear over the clamor of the crowd, and he gestured down at the chained citizens. A glimmer of light behind him caught Alex's eye, and she spotted Dr. Hoshi rolling up her sleeves.

As much as Alex wanted the doctor to blast Marcus into oblivion, she couldn't risk any innocent people being hurt, even if they *were* acting like fools. And she couldn't risk compromising Supergirl's mission. If they gave Marcus any reason to be suspicious, it was all over.

Alex shook her head, and Dr. Hoshi placed her hands in her lap.

The doors to the lion cages sprang open, and Marcus smiled deviously. "Ladies and gentlemen, let the games begin!"

13

MARCUS SMILED DEVIOUSLY AT Supergirl. "How do I look, love?"

"Like I want to punch you," she said, smiling back.

J'onn had assumed Marcus's form, and now he and Supergirl waited for Mon-El, James, Jason, and Claude to change into uniforms they'd borrowed from a few bound and gagged sentries.

Just like Alex's team, Supergirl and company had embarked on their mission at sunup. Supergirl had occasionally used her superhearing to follow the parade, and when the sound of cheering bystanders grew exponentially louder, Supergirl knew the procession had reached the coliseum. That's when she'd led the guards to an alley ambush.

Her four friends emerged from a darkened shop, making last-minute adjustments to their uniforms and weapons.

"What do you think?" asked Mon-El, showing off his uniform.

"I think all four of you will pass just fine," J'onn said with an approving nod. "Are we ready to begin?"

"I have been ready since yesterday," said Claude. Even when his helmet hadn't been casting a shadow over his eyes, they'd been marked with dark circles. The poor violinist had stayed awake all night watching the estate for anything suspicious.

"And you haven't noticed anything strange going on at Marcus's estate?" Supergirl asked to confirm that fact.

Claude shook his head. "I heard nothing, I saw nothing, and Marcus left this morning with his bodyguards. He did look upset, though."

"No doubt because Hannah wasn't going with him," said Jason.

J'onn turned to Supergirl. "How go the games?"

She tilted her head to one side and listened.

. . . *delirium, she has asked that I not harm any of the beasts you see here today.*

"Sounds like Hannah talked Marcus into not hurting any animals during the show," she said. "That's a relief."

"Won't that make for a dull opening?" asked James.

Supergirl shrugged. "I'm sure they'll find a way to spice

it up. The important thing is that Marcus is fully distracted, so it's safe to move in."

J'onn held up a pair of green restraints. "Time for the 'kryptonite' handcuffs."

Supergirl held her arms in front of her. Had the cuffs been real kryptonite, she'd have already been on her knees, but these were harmless iron painted a metallic green.

J'onn fastened them around her wrists, and Claude and Jason each grabbed one of her arms, with Mon-El and James marching behind.

"Remember," Supergirl said to Claude, "as soon as Hannah destroys her altar, you get her out of the estate."

Claude nodded and took a deep breath. "I am ready."

J'onn marched jauntily in front of them toward the estate with Supergirl stumbling between Claude and Jason, who half carried, half dragged her. Mon-El and James brought up the rear, occasionally prodding Supergirl in the back with their swords.

As they approached the entrance, Marcus's real guards watched them curiously with weapons half raised.

"Aedile Marcus," one of the guards addressed J'onn. "You should be at the coliseum."

"I was on my way," said J'onn. "But my field soldiers found someone trying to sneak into the estate." He glanced smugly at Supergirl. "So before I head back, I thought I'd give her a grand tour of my cellar. You know how I love a captive audience."

The guards chuckled and sneered at Supergirl.

"Of course, Aedile Marcus."

They stepped aside, and J'onn led the way into the estate.

This was going even better than Supergirl had hoped.

Hannah was pacing the floor in the receiving room, and when she saw them, she instinctively made a beeline for Claude. J'onn stepped into her path and held out his arms.

"Valeria, my love. How are you feeling?"

Hannah regarded J'onn with wide eyes, no doubt wary of his likeness to Marcus, but when he bent to kiss her cheek, Supergirl heard J'onn whisper his identity into her ear.

"I . . . I'm still feeling a bit under the weather," she told J'onn when he pulled away. "I see you've brought company."

J'onn looked down his nose at Supergirl. "Yes, I will imprison her so she can't ruin my plans." He took Hannah's hands. "Would you care to come? I know she frightens you, and I want you to see her safely locked up."

"I'd like that very much." Hannah looped her arm through J'onn's, and he nodded to Mon-El, James, Jason, and Claude. "Bring her." J'onn jerked his head in Supergirl's direction, and the men dragged her toward the cellar.

"You won't get away with this," Supergirl said in a weak voice. "My friends will stop you."

"I expect they'll try, but they'll fail miserably," said J'onn. He pointed to the guards at the top of the cellar steps. "I want anyone down below brought up to watch the outside perimeter. We'll no doubt have company soon."

The guards glanced at one another, and J'onn crossed his arms.

"Is there a problem?" he asked. "Because I can have you replaced. Body *and* soul."

One of the guards sprinted down the cellar stairs, calling to others below. His counterpart headed for the front door.

Supergirl felt Jason's fingers tighten around her.

"I don't like this," he said in a soft voice. "Something feels . . . off."

"Like it's too easy?" mumbled Mon-El.

Jason shook his head. "Magic. Strong magic."

"Probably the curses," said J'onn under his breath.

Supergirl heard footsteps pounding up the stairs.

"Quiet. They're coming," she said.

J'onn leaned against the cellar doorframe and stared at the fingernails on one hand. "Any day now, gentlemen," he said as the sentries hurried past. As the last one lumbered up the steps, J'onn asked, "Is that everyone?"

"Yes, Aedile Marcus," said the heavyset guard. "But that leaves nobody watching the—"

J'onn held up a hand. "I've got four very capable men with me. We'll be fine."

"Yes, Aedile Marcus. Excuse me." The guard pushed past J'onn, who had to step down into the cellar to let him pass.

There was a faint buzzing sound, and suddenly Supergirl found herself staring at Martian Manhunter.

J'onn had lost his Marcus disguise.

"Oh, crap," she whispered.

Everyone in the room turned toward the buzzing sound, and upon seeing J'onn, the guards shouted and rushed toward the cellar door. Mon-El pushed the guard at the top of the stairs aside, Jason and Claude released Supergirl, and James raised his sword.

"I knew it!" said Jason, reaching for his dagger. "The cellar entrance was booby-trapped."

"Looks like we'll be fighting our way downstairs," said Supergirl.

She yanked on the chain between her cuffed wrists, snapping the links like dried twigs.

Shouting obscenities, a soldier charged at her, and Supergirl raised one of her arms, blocking his blade with a cuff. Her free hand shot out and knocked him backward into another soldier. She turned her head just in time to see a spear flying at her.

J'onn, still in Martian Manhunter form, reached out and snatched the spear from the air. He swung it in a wide arc, striking a sentry on the back of the skull and bringing the spear down and around for another pass to sweep the legs out from under a sentry who'd just arrived.

"Six guards inside and six guards out, right, Jason?" asked Supergirl.

Jason smashed his forehead against a sentry's nose and nodded. "Five down, seven to go."

"James, Mon-El, and I will handle the guards up here," J'onn told Supergirl. "You, Jason, Hannah, and Claude get to the cellar and destroy those altars."

Supergirl nodded and beckoned to Hannah and Claude, who were huddled together behind James and his shield.

"We've got work to do," Supergirl said, ushering them down the cellar steps ahead of her.

She followed, and Jason brought up the rear, closing the door behind them.

"You really think that door is keeping anyone out?" Supergirl asked.

"No, but if there are more booby traps down here, especially explosive ones, it might protect your friends upstairs from harm," said Jason. He pointed down a corridor lined with bronze statues and oil-lit sconces. "The altars are this way," he said, stepping around Hannah and Claude.

Even though all the guards had left, Supergirl found herself walking with fists clenched and ears perked for suspicious sounds.

The corridor curved to the right, and Jason paused outside a door. "I sense magic here. You might want to step back."

Hannah and Claude nearly tripped over Supergirl in their hurry to get away.

Jason ran his fingers over the door, speaking softly. The handle of the door glowed a brilliant blue, and he chuckled.

"Marcus is a formidable adversary. This is a frost lock," said Jason. "Anyone who touches the door handle would instantly freeze from the inside out."

"What happens if we touch the rest of the door?" asked Supergirl.

"Nothing."

"I was hoping you'd say that." Supergirl kicked it down.

The open doorway led to a small room with two stone altars at its center. Supergirl wasn't sure why, but she'd been expecting altars as large as the one outside the temple. Yet these were no bigger than shoe boxes. Upon each rested a chalice filled with red liquid.

"What is this?" asked Claude.

"You don't want to know," said Supergirl. She glanced at Jason. "Which altar do you think is Hannah's?"

He ran his hands over the stone of each. "This one," he said, pointing to the altar on the left. "I can feel where Marcus carved her initials."

"Um . . . you said I have to destroy my altar." Hannah examined the stone. "But how am I supposed to do that? I don't have superstrength."

"You don't need it," said Jason. He picked up the chalice and poured the contents onto the floor in a circle around the altar. Then he reached for his dagger and handed it to Hannah. "Drive the point of this into the altar."

Hannah gave him a dubious look but raised the dagger and brought it down hard against the stone. The blade pierced the rock and buried itself to the hilt. She wiggled the dagger from side to side, and as she did so, Supergirl felt the ground rumble beneath her feet.

"You've almost got it!" Claude said. "Hit it again!"

Taking a deep breath, Hannah withdrew the dagger and drove it into the stone a second time. The ground shook even harder as the altar crumbled to pieces. A wisp of shadow emerged from Hannah's body and vanished with a sigh.

Hannah smiled and touched a hand to her chest. "She's gone. Valeria's gone."

Claude cheered and hugged Hannah tightly, almost losing his balance as the ground shook for a third time.

"Someone's not happy we're down here," Supergirl said to Jason, but he was too busy pouring a potion over the altar pieces and chanting.

Supergirl grabbed Hannah and Claude by their arms. "Time for you to go."

Hannah gripped Supergirl's hands and squeezed. "Thank you. For everything."

"Yes, thank you so much," said Claude, running from the room with Hannah.

Supergirl turned to Jason.

"It's done," he said. "Now—"

There was a blood-curdling scream from beyond the doorway, and Supergirl's skin broke out in goose bumps.

"Hannah," she whispered, running out of the chamber and down the corridor.

"Supergirl, wait! Your altar!" Jason shouted after her.

But she didn't have time to think about that.

Because Claude was lying unconscious on the ground, and . . . one of the bronze statues held Hannah at sword point.

When the rest of the bronze statues saw Supergirl, they leaped from their pedestals and ran toward her, various weapons at the ready.

"Oh, ho, you do *not* want to go up against me," she said, planting her feet as the nearest statue swung its sword. As she'd done before, Supergirl raised an arm to block the strike, but the sword sliced easily through the metal cuff and slashed Supergirl's flesh.

"Holy—" She bit her lip and glanced at her arm. Blood was dripping from her ripped sleeve.

Jason ran up behind her. "I told you, you're vulnerable to magic! What do you think brought these statues to life?" He jerked her out of the way just as the statue swung its sword again.

"Hey!" she shouted at it. "You're a statue! That means you don't move!"

Supergirl unleashed her freeze breath on the statue's arm. With a crackling of ice, it froze in place.

Unfortunately, the statue had another perfectly good arm.

It punched Supergirl soundly in the side of the head, sending her crashing into a cellar wall.

Light appeared at the top of the cellar stairs, and J'onn's legs came into view. "Supergirl? Are you—"

"No! Get back!" she cried as a bronze archer fired a trio of flaming arrows at Martian Manhunter.

Supergirl cringed, knowing his fear of fire, and, sure enough, J'onn stood rooted to the spot as the balls of flame hurtled toward him. Supergirl staggered to her feet and tried to force her way through the statues, but at least twenty of them stood between her and her friend.

A knife to the back of one of her thighs brought her to her knees, and all she could do was shout, "J'onn! Move!"

Luckily, James and Mon-El appeared at that moment, and James thrust his shield in front of J'onn. The flaming arrows bounced off its surface and fell to the ground. Mon-El leaped down the stairs and stomped on the flames while

James snapped his fingers to break J'onn out of his stupor.

"Let's get in there!" he shouted.

Mon-El had already dashed into the fray, grabbing one of the statues around the waist and turning it to fight its own kind.

"Be careful!" Supergirl shouted to Mon-El. "I'm vulnerable to magic, and you might be, too!"

As if to prove her point, the statue Mon-El was holding kicked back, catching him in the shin. Mon-El dropped the statue, cursing, and aimed a kick of his own at the statue's side. James ran past and tugged Mon-El to one side just as a different, axe-wielding statue tried to decapitate the Daxamite.

Meanwhile, the archer readied another trio of fiery arrows. Supergirl used her freeze breath again and extinguished the flames while J'onn crushed the entire quiver. Then, Supergirl fixed her gaze on the statue's bow, blasting it with her heat vision until it softened and bent beyond use. Unfortunately, magical metal took more effort to melt than regular metal, and Supergirl could already feel her head starting to throb.

Amid all the chaos, Hannah was still being held by a statue, sword at her throat, as she shouted to wake Claude.

Supergirl glanced back at Jason. "How do we stop these things?"

Jason pointed above her. Supergirl rolled out of the way just as an axe struck the ground where she'd been kneeling.

She fought the statue for control of its axe while using her heat vision on its legs.

"I know a way to stop them." Jason jammed his dagger into a statue's shoulder. "But you're not going to like it."

"Oh, I like pretty much anything more than this," Supergirl said, yanking the axe from its owner's hands. She tossed the axe to Mon-El, who swung it and beheaded two statues in one blow.

Jason parried his statue's attack and plunged his dagger into its chest. "Very well," he said while the statue fell. "But remember what a great guy I am."

Jason sheathed his dagger and dropped to his knees.

"Wait. What?" Supergirl grappled with a statue that lunged at Jason. "OK, I was wrong. I definitely don't like what you're doing!"

Jason closed his eyes and placed his hands on the floor.

"Change! Change, O' form of man," he said. "Release the might from fleshy mire! Boil the blood in heart of fire!"

Jason's voice boomed through the corridor. The bronze statues all paused and watched him. So did James, J'onn, Mon-El, and Supergirl.

With his back hunched, Jason roared, "Gone! Gone! The form of man! Rise, the demon Etrigan!"

Supergirl stared, wide-eyed, as the Jason Blood she knew disappeared and a fiery-eyed, yellow-skinned, horned demon took his place.

"Alex," she whispered. "You are missing *all* the excitement."

14

A S SOON AS THE DOORS TO THE lion cages opened, Alex turned to the other people on the chain. They were all screaming and backing away.

"Listen!" She waved her arms. "Nobody panic. If we run—"

She'd been about to say, *If we run, they'll chase us,* but the first part of her sentence sounded like a good enough idea to the others.

"Run!" one of them cried, and they all sprinted for an archway on the opposite side of the arena.

Alex was jerked off her feet and dragged through the sand. Over her shoulder, she could see the lions leaving their cages. They sniffed the air and watched the humans run for a moment.

Then all six lions gave chase.

"Wait!" Alex coughed and gagged on the dust from the scrambling feet in front of her. "Everyone . . . stop!" she choked out, yanking on the chains.

But nineteen people pulling against her were too strong, and she had no choice but to skid along behind them until they stopped at the archway. A heavy iron gate had been drawn across it.

"It's closed!" someone shouted as Alex got to her feet.

Before they could take off again, she wove a section of chain through the gate. She had zero desire to eat any more dirt.

"What are you doing?" A man tried to push her aside, and Alex twisted his arm behind his back.

"You need to calm down!" she barked into his ear. "All of you."

"The masked man is trying to kill us!" someone else screamed, and pointed at Alex. "He's chained us to the gate!"

A roar quickly returned their attention to the lions, which had slowed to a walk and were sauntering toward the archway. The people on the chain faced the lions, and the lions growled low in their throats, tails swishing from side to side. But they didn't come any closer.

Retreating prey could easily be picked off one by one. But when the people stood together . . .

"The lions know they're outnumbered," Alex said to nobody in particular. "And that we could beat them."

Could beat them, if Alex managed to convince the others on the chain to work as a team. Already they were falling into chaos, screaming and fumbling to untangle the chain from the gate. Several people had turned their backs on the lions, giving a welcome opportunity to attack.

There was still slack left in the chain, so Alex gripped a section in one hand and swung it in front of her, shouting at the lions.

"HA! GET BACK!"

The closest lions balked and retreated. The others paced side to side, watching her.

"We outnumber them!" she shouted over her shoulder. "And they know it."

"But they have sharp claws and teeth!" someone countered.

"And we have a really long chain," said Alex. She glanced across the arena. "And cages! We can get them back into the cages!"

"Are you insane?" someone else asked. "There's no way we can get the lions to do what we want."

Alex whipped the chain at a lion who was getting too close. "You people dragged me all the way over here, and *I* didn't want to do that. We're stronger together than you realize!"

"But you have armor. We have nothing!" a woman complained.

"Oh, for the love of—" Alex pulled off her helmet and handed it to the woman. "Here."

The rest of the people on the chain stared at Alex. The audience stared at Alex.

Then the noise from the audience magnified a hundredfold.

"The masked man is a woman!"

"I don't believe it!"

"She's giving her helmet to someone else!"

"She's so brave!"

Half the audience was cheering, half was jeering, but all were thoroughly enthralled.

An older man at the front of the chain stepped away from the group and closer to the lions, holding his spare section of chain the way Alex did.

"The young woman is right!" he declared. "We work together, or we wait for them to kill us one by one." He twirled his chain in a figure eight on one end, while Alex swung hers on the other. She unwove the rest of the chain from the fence and breathed a sigh of relief when nobody bolted.

The people on the chain, however, crowded close to either the old man or to Alex.

"No," said Alex, stepping away from the others. "We have to spread out and make ourselves look like an army. Confuse the lions!"

Reluctantly, the other people did so, shouting and waving their arms as they slowly approached the beasts. The lions roared but retreated still farther, one of them even breaking into a run to escape the mass of people.

"It's working!" someone said.

On Alex's command, they shifted to the left to herd one of the lions into its cage. As soon as the lion was inside, the older man at the front of the chain lifted the cage door and secured it to a chorus of *"Booo!"* from the crowd.

"You want to come down here and trade places with us?" Alex called to the crowd.

She glanced at Marcus for his reaction, but he'd turned away from the arena to listen to a man waving emphatically. Alex had a feeling the conversation was about her sister.

"Let's hurry this up, folks!" she said to the other people on the chain.

More slowly than she'd hoped, they herded the lions into their cages, and when the last beast was put away and the noise from the crowd was deafening, Alex turned to Marcus's booth once more.

But he was no longer there.

Alex cursed under her breath and looked to where Dr. Hoshi was sitting. The doctor was applauding and whistling with her fingers until Alex pointed out Marcus's empty seat.

Wide-eyed, Dr. Hoshi leaped to her feet and pushed her way through the people sitting in her row, headed for the ramp that led to the lower level.

"Come on," Alex told the people on the chain. "A friend of mine is going to get us out of here."

She and the others ran toward the northern archway, reaching it just as Dr. Hoshi did.

"Step back!" she told them, thrusting a hand at the gate's lock.

A blast of white light shot from her palm, and the lock fell to the ground with a *thunk*.

She and Alex slid the gate open and hugged.

"That was spectacular!" said Dr. Hoshi. "Alex Danvers: lion tamer." She leaned closer. "And crazy person tamer."

Alex smiled as the people with her hugged one another. "They weren't crazy. Just scared." She held her cuffed wrists up to Dr. Hoshi. "Can you take care of these?"

Dr. Hoshi sucked in her breath. "I've been training a lot, but I can't promise perfect aim."

At that moment, a hand appeared over Dr. Hoshi's shoulder, jingling a set of keys.

Dr. Hoshi turned and Winn smirked at her and Alex, twirling the key ring on one finger. Alex hugged him tight.

She stepped back and held out her wrists so Winn could unlock the cuffs. "Winn Schott, you never cease to— Look out!" she cried as a coliseum guard leaped to put Winn in a choke hold.

Unfortunately, choke holds weren't one of the things Alex and James had trained Winn on. Alex tugged at the chains still linking her to the others and glanced at Dr. Hoshi, hoping for a moment of perfect aim.

But Winn seemed to have his own exit strategy.

He tightened his grip on one of the keys and stabbed backward and upward, poking the guard in the face. The guard screamed and released Winn. While the guard stumbled about, Winn placed his helmet behind the guard's feet and pushed against the man's chest. The guard fell backward over the helmet, landing hard enough to shake the floorboards. He groaned and waved an arm but made no further effort to move.

"Huh. What do you know? David *did* take down Goliath," said Alex as Dr. Hoshi clapped.

Winn rolled his eyes, having no doubt understood the names, and held up the key ring.

Alex extended her wrists.

"If Marcus is gone and National City still looks like Ancient Rome, I'm guessing Supergirl and the others ran into some trouble," said Dr. Hoshi while Winn unlocked Alex.

"Looks like," Alex said with a terse nod. She massaged her now free wrists. "Which means we have to get out of here and help them. Fast. Where can we find some horses?"

Dr. Hoshi smiled. "I might have a quicker way to get us there. If you trust me."

"Of course," said Alex as Dr. Hoshi pushed back the hood of her cloak and removed her blond wig.

"We're going to need a little more space." The doctor stepped into the arena. "Don't forget to grab Winn."

"Winn!" Alex snapped her fingers to get his attention, and he passed the keys to one of the prisoners before following her into the arena. "OK, Doc. What's up?"

In answer, Dr. Hoshi held her arms out from her sides and slowly lifted off the ground.

Alex gasped. "You can fly?"

Dr. Hoshi tilted her hand from side to side. "I can travel on light. That's the secret project I've been working on with J'onn: learning to control my powers."

Winn laughed and clapped.

Dr. Hoshi held a hand out to him, and he instantly stopped clapping.

"Ha-ha . . . no." Winn crossed his arms, still smiling.

Dr. Hoshi dropped back to the ground. "Oh, come on, Winn. See how easily I landed?" She indicated her feet. "Right side up and everything."

"The only thing he's going to understand is being left behind," said Alex. "That, and . . . Kara." She looked at Winn and drew a finger across her throat, shaking her head.

Winn paled but closed his eyes and reached for Dr. Hoshi.

She put one arm around him and one around Alex, who smirked.

"You know, just a couple of days ago, you were terrified to fly," Alex reminded her.

"What can I say?" Dr. Hoshi said with a smile. "You get used to it."

They lifted off the ground, and before Alex could ask Dr. Hoshi how fast she could go, they were already halfway to Marcus's estate.

Alex clenched her jaw and tightened her grip.

Hang on, Kara, she thought. *I'm coming.*

15

SUPERGIRL HAD SEEN SOME STRANGE creatures in her past, but she couldn't take her eyes off Etrigan, her very first demon. With every exhale, smoke spewed from his nostrils, and his smile revealed a sharp set of fangs.

She hoped to Rao that the demon was on her side.

"Uh . . . hello." Supergirl extended a hand. "I'm—"

"Supergirl. The Girl of Steel," he said in a deep, gravelly voice. "With still more names you won't reveal."

She withdrew her hand. "Okay, you know me. And you rhyme. Both unsettling."

Behind her, metal clashed against metal as the bronze statues renewed their battle against Mon-El, James, and J'onn. Supergirl whirled around, poised to fight.

"Come on, Etrigan. Let's do this!"

She used her freeze breath on an encroaching statue and smashed the dagger out of its hand. Etrigan didn't move.

"Etrigan?" She glanced over her shoulder. "A little help here!"

The demon cocked his head to one side, studying Supergirl and the chaos behind her.

"Such a quandary I find myself in," he said. "To roast you alive or save your skin."

"Are you serious?" Supergirl flipped a bronze statue over her shoulder and scowled at Etrigan. "I let you keep my apple!"

Etrigan chuckled, the sound like lava rocks scraping together. "My outer shell, not me, you see. Although without him, I *would* expire." Etrigan sighed and cracked his knuckles. "Duck if you wish. Here comes the fire."

"What?" Supergirl asked as Etrigan opened his mouth, which danced with flames. "Whoa!"

Supergirl pressed her back to the wall as Etrigan shot an orange blaze down the corridor from his mouth *and* hands. She chanced a look at the statues in range of his infernal attack. The bronze figures glowed red-hot and slowly began to dissolve into molten pools.

The fire died down, and Etrigan stared at Supergirl. "Tarry no longer, lest I include your precious kin in my turpitude," he said, stalking toward the rest of the statues.

Supergirl's eyes widened, and she zipped down the hall, grabbing Hannah and the statue holding her hostage. Everyone in Supergirl's flight path, bronze and human alike, dove out of the way.

"James, grab Claude! Mon-El, grab J'onn!" she shouted, for in the face of Etrigan's fire, the Green Martian had frozen again. "Then everyone get out of here!"

She zipped up the cellar stairs and dropped Hannah and the statue on the floor. Hannah scrambled away as Supergirl wrestled the statue for its sword.

"In case you didn't know," she said, blasting the statue's sword hand with her heat vision, "the Bronze Age is over."

The statue's fingers softened, losing their grip on the weapon, and Supergirl snatched it away, flinging the statue in one direction and the sword in another.

"Whoa! Watch where you throw that thing!" Alex sidestepped the sword as it hurtled toward her. She, Winn, and Dr. Hoshi were standing in the foyer.

"Alex!" Supergirl limped toward her sister and hugged her tightly. "And Winn! *And* Dr. Hoshi!" She extended an arm and folded them into the hug. "I'm so glad you're all OK!"

"*I'm* so glad to be around people who understand me," said Winn.

"Hey! I understand you . . . now," said Alex.

"We brought you a souvenir," said Dr. Hoshi, handing Supergirl a cloth bag.

Supergirl opened it and peered at the pale yellow granules inside. "Millet?"

"You know this stuff?" Alex asked in surprise.

Supergirl nodded. "My old boss, Cat, ate it for a week during one of her health kicks. I found kernels *everywhere* in her office." Supergirl jiggled the contents and thought. "Actually, this might come in handy."

"Glad to hear it," said Alex. "Because Marcus is coming, so you'd better—" She frowned at Supergirl, who was now balancing her weight on one leg. "Kryptonite?"

Supergirl shook her head. "Magic. Apparently, I'm vulnerable to it."

"Those swords are magical?" Winn pointed at the one she'd flung across the room.

"And their owners," said Supergirl just as Mon-El appeared at the top of the cellar steps with a slightly dazed J'onn.

"Agent Danvers!" he said with a look of relief. "Agent Hoshi, Agent Schott." J'onn nodded to all of them. "Our mission isn't over yet."

As if to prove his point, Claude stumbled up the steps

with James right behind, two more statues clambering to get past his shield.

"I'm on it," said Alex.

She picked up the sword Supergirl had flung aside and dashed off to help James.

"Winn, Dr. Hoshi"—Supergirl looked at them both—"I need you to get Claude and Hannah out of here and as far away as possible."

The agents chased after the couple, who were arm in arm and already running for an exit.

A spine-chilling shriek sounded from the cellar, and Supergirl spun on her heel, zooming back down the stairs. She passed pools of molten bronze, but the demon who'd caused them was nowhere in sight.

"Etrigan!" Supergirl called, rounding a corner.

She halted in midair, hovering over Etrigan and . . .

"Marcus." Supergirl's lip curled as she dropped to the ground.

The patrician was holding a dripping jug above Etrigan's fallen form. "Did you know," he said, "that there's an underground tunnel between the concert hall that stood here and City Hall? It's meant for shuttling celebrities between locations. It's also excellent for sneaking up on unsuspecting demons with holy water."

"Very cowardly," Supergirl said, crossing her arms. "Valeria would be proud . . . well, would've been proud if she was still here."

Marcus scowled. "Yes, you've ripped her from her body."

"*Hannah Nesmith's* body," Supergirl corrected. "Valeria's back where she belongs. You never should have resurrected her. It wasn't right."

"'Right'?" Marcus spoke the word through clenched teeth. "'RIGHT'? Who are you to dole out judgment?"

Marcus tilted the jug forward until the holy water splashed Etrigan's cheek. The demon screamed as his flesh reddened, steam curling from the wound. Supergirl knocked the water jug from Marcus's hand and crouched beside Etrigan.

"Stop! You're hurting him!"

"Aw." Marcus struck a tone of mock endearment. "What a cute couple you'd make. Demon and dullard." He strolled a few paces away. "Supergirl—or Kara, when you wear those ridiculous glasses—you're the strongest woman on Earth. But tell me, what are you without your strength?"

Supergirl glowered, gripping the back of her wounded leg as she followed him. "More than good enough to defeat you."

Marcus laughed mirthlessly. "Really? Look at you now, limping along." His face became serious. "I'd love to kill you, but I made a deal with Tempus. So instead I'll kill all those you hold dear."

Supergirl circled him slowly. "And how do you plan to do that? We're stronger together than—"

Marcus rolled his eyes. "Ugh. 'Stronger together. Stronger together.' Enough of that." He gestured to the floor at his feet, where a circle had been painted. "Do you know what this is?"

"A circle," said Supergirl.

"Oh, for the love . . . *yes*, very well done." He clapped sarcastically. "Do you know what *kind* of circle?" Marcus waited half a second before answering his own question. "It's a summoning circle. They're all over the place." He pointed down the corridor. "Which means I can summon as many demons as I want to do my bidding." Marcus narrowed his eyes. "And my bidding begins with destroying your loved ones."

Supergirl stepped toward him. "You wouldn't."

Marcus pressed two fingers against her sternum and nudged her against a wall.

Instantly the sconces there wrapped around her arms, holding her in place.

"Can't have you interrupting me," Marcus said.

Then he began chanting.

Etrigan shifted on the ground nearby. "Supergirl . . ."

Supergirl struggled against the magical metal that bound her arms. "Marcus! Stop!"

Marcus raised his voice and continued the chant.

"You're going to regret this!" Supergirl shouted.

Marcus's voice dropped to a whisper and then fell silent as his summoning spell came to its end.

"Welp. I tried to warn him," Supergirl said, clucking her tongue.

Then she lifted her uninjured leg and stomped on the floor. Hard.

Directly beneath her foot, the tile crumbled, and cracks branched out from the epicenter.

Cracks that spread all the way to Marcus's summoning circle.

Marcus looked down and let out an anguished cry. "You stupid girl! You broke the circle!"

"I did?" Supergirl feigned disbelief. "Huh. Guess I don't know my own strength."

"Idiot! The demon is free to do what it wants!" Marcus glanced nervously at the broken circle, from which gray mist was now rising. "My only hope is to summon another."

He turned away from the circle and collided with an invisible wall.

"What—" Marcus pressed out with his hands but couldn't break through. "What is this?"

Supergirl gazed at the ceiling. "Let's see. Dullard, stupid girl, and . . . what was the last thing you called me? Idiot?" She locked eyes with Marcus. "And yet, somehow, I managed to outsmart you."

Marcus peeked over his shoulder at the thickening mist he'd summoned and then turned back to Supergirl with an expression of sheer terror. "You trapped me!"

"I did. Thanks for the bag of millet, by the way," she said. "It came in handy."

Marcus glanced down and saw what Supergirl had been doing while she was clutching her injured leg: using the millet to make a circle around *his* circle.

"The fun thing about millet," said Supergirl, "is that those tiny grains can fit in the tiniest crevices. Between office floorboards, under couch cushions . . . even into the cracks someone just put in the ground." She smiled smugly at Marcus. "They really fill any gaps nicely. And that's why *my* circle never broke."

Marcus paled, and Supergirl tapped her chin.

"Now, correct me if I'm wrong," she said. "But if your

circle's broken and *mine* is whole and *you're* trapped inside," doesn't that mean *I'm* in control of the demon?"

A gigantic maw filled with crooked white teeth emerged from the mist, along with two gangly arms that reached for Marcus.

"Help me!" Marcus called out to Supergirl.

She pressed her lips together and stared at the ceiling some more. "I don't know . . . what you did was pretty unforgivable."

Marcus dropped to his knees, pulling at the demon's hands, which had wrapped around his throat. "Please! Supergirl!"

She looked down at Marcus. "When this is over, you'll go peacefully and quietly to jail."

He nodded emphatically.

"And you'll never summon another demon," she added.

"Never," Marcus choked out.

Supergirl nodded in satisfaction. "What's this demon's name?"

"I AM BAYTOR!" roared the demon.

Supergirl raised an eyebrow. "All right, then, Baytor, take your hands off Marcus," she commanded.

"Awww," said Baytor. But he let Marcus go and Marcus collapsed on the floor, gasping for air.

Supergirl jerked her head toward the sconces holding her. "Baytor, remove my restraints."

The demon waggled his fingers, and the iron around Supergirl's arms disappeared.

She crouched beside Etrigan and rolled him onto his back. He groaned and blinked at her.

"Jason?" Supergirl asked. "I know you're in there. It's time to trade places with Etrigan."

Etrigan swallowed and nodded. "Gone now, O' Etrigan. And rise again, the form of man."

The demon's yellow ochre lightened to a peach tone, his features transforming into those of Jason Blood. Jason blinked a few times and sat up.

"Welcome back," said Supergirl with a smile. "I could use your help with a few things."

While Jason banished Baytor, and the DEO agents dragged Marcus out of the cellar, Supergirl removed the offering from her altar and smashed the stone into pebbles.

"There's something you should know before we banish Tempus Fugit," Jason told her, entering the room. "Reversing the curse will also reverse time to just before Tempus was called."

Supergirl's forehead wrinkled. "So Marcus could potentially summon him again?"

"Yes. And"—Jason held up a finger—"with time reset, all actions and *memories* will be undone . . . except yours, since your blood was used for the summoning."

Supergirl nodded. "I understand."

Jason extended a hand. "It was a pleasure working with you, Supergirl." He smiled at her. "Kara Danvers."

"Nope." She grinned and opened her arms. "That's not how I say good-bye to my friends, Etrigan. Jason Blood."

They hugged, and Supergirl stepped back, rubbing her hands together in anticipation.

"OK! Let's end this," she said.

Jason poured the potion over the broken pieces of her altar and chanted. Once again, the entire room shook, from floor to walls to ceiling. The second Jason ended his chant, a flash of white light burst from the altar remains.

Supergirl threw her right arm up to shield her eyes and stumbled backward. A pair of hands grabbed her by the waist to keep her from falling.

"Whoa, Kara! Are you OK?" asked Mon-El.

Kara lowered her arm and blinked to adjust to the

darkness of the night sky. She glanced down at herself, at the pink sweater she'd been wearing four days earlier, when Caesar's Comet arrived.

"Uh . . . yeah." She fiddled with her glasses. "Sorry, I felt a little dizzy for a second."

"Don't be embarrassed." Dr. Hoshi looked over from where she stood in front of the telescope. "Heights make me dizzy sometimes, too. That's why I hate flying."

"Yeah, but Kara does it all the time," Alex said, giving her sister a worried look. "Are you sure you're OK?"

Kara held up a finger. "Hold that thought."

Leaping into the sky, Kara sped toward National City Music Hall, punching her way through the sidewalk behind it and landing in the underground tunnel. She took four steps around a corner and kicked down the door there.

On the other side of it, Marcus was scrambling away from the flying debris. In his hands he clutched two familiar-looking goblets, no doubt meant for the two stone altars Kara saw at the center of the room.

Marcus stared at Kara, wide-eyed. "Supe . . . I mean . . . uh . . ."

"Save it," she said, smashing the altars with her fists. "Also, the music hall doesn't allow outside food or drink, so I'll just take those." Kara snatched the goblets from Marcus and blasted them with her heat vision until the contents were reduced to steam.

Marcus's mouth opened and closed several times, but he made no move to stop her. "How did you—"

Kara grabbed him by the front of his shirt and slammed him against a wall. Marcus squirmed and tried to free himself, but even with all his strength, he had nothing against an angry and adrenaline-fueled Kara.

"Let's get one thing straight," she said. "Earth is my home. National City is my home. And there is nothing alien, human, *or* demon that will cause it harm. Because I will protect this city at all costs." She brought her face to within an inch of his. "Every. Time."

Marcus blinked at her. "Is this because I used to call you Carka?"

"Ugh!" Kara slammed her forehead against his, and Marcus passed out cold.

"You've been around for over two thousand years, and that's your best comeback?" she asked his unconscious form. "Well, luckily, you'll have a lifetime to think of a better one." Kara hoisted him onto one shoulder. "In prison."

As she walked down the corridor, she hummed Hannah's melody to herself.

It was shaping up to be a very interesting week.

Again.

EPILOGUE

"**K**ARA, THESE SEATS ARE FAN-tastic!" Lena Luthor gazed, wide-eyed, at the stage where the orchestra musicians were warming up. "Thank you so much for inviting me to join you."

"Of course!" Kara smiled at her. "When Hannah offered me front-row tickets to her performance, I couldn't think of anyone else I'd rather take." She bumped Lena's shoulder with her own.

Plus, it's my way of thanking you for your help in the Rome Dome, Kara thought to herself. *Even if you don't remember.*

Just as Jason had said, nobody else seemed aware of

what had transpired during the missing week. But there were little hints that somewhere in their subconscious they knew.

Alex had become increasingly vocal about getting more women into the DEO, Mon-El insisted on watching *Terminator,* Winn had asked James to teach him a few self-defense moves, even J'onn had started reading a copy of Ovid's *Metamorphoses* . . . in Latin.

Dr. Hoshi had, unfortunately, lost her power to control light, but since she wasn't aware she'd had it, she'd been blissfully planning a trip to an observatory in Japan.

"Excuse us," a woman said in a thick Spanish accent. "We'd like to get past."

"Of course," said Kara.

She and Lena stood, leaning back against their seats to let a tall, dark-haired woman and her auburn-haired male companion slip by. Kara caught a glimpse of white in the man's hair and did a double take.

"Jason?"

He turned and gave her a curious look. "Um . . . hello."

She pointed to herself. "It's Kara! We . . ." Then a realization struck her. "We've never met, but I'm a big fan of yours." She adjusted her glasses and offered a nervous smile.

Jason Blood nodded politely. "Well, thank you. It's always nice to meet a fan."

Kara dropped into her seat, her cheeks warm with embarrassment.

"You have fans?" she heard the Hispanic woman ask Jason. "I'm impressed."

He waved her off. "You should talk, Tlaca." In a softer voice, he added, "Doesn't being a princess come with an entire kingdom of fans?"

Kara's eyebrows went up at the word "princess."

"Royal subjects are not the same as fans," Tlaca told Jason. "I would like to be adored, not worshiped."

"Sorry," Kara said, twisting in her seat, "I couldn't help but overhear." She lowered her voice. "Are you a princess? Because I write for *CatCo* magazine, and I'd love to interview you."

"Oh!" Tlaca pressed a hand to her heart. "I'm flattered, but I'm heading to Central City tomorrow. Next time I'm in town, though."

Kara handed her a business card. "Kara Danvers. The offer always stands."

"*I* didn't get that offer." Jason scowled at Tlaca. "Look. Now you've taken my one fan."

Tlaca laughed again. "Please, Jason. Who would really be a fan of demonology?"

He shrugged and opened his performance program. "Maybe Supergirl."

Kara gawked at Jason, who continued to study his booklet. But she could've sworn the corner of his mouth twitched with a smile.

Tlaca slapped him on the knee. "Jason, you are too much!" She winked at Kara. "You are better off being a fan of mine."

Lena appeared over Kara's shoulder. "Oh, around here we're all fans of Supergirl."

Tlaca tilted her head to one side. "I hear that from a lot of people in this city. This Supergirl is powerful?"

"Some say she's the strongest woman on Earth," said Kara.

"Good," said Tlaca with a nod. "You can introduce us when I return."

"Uh . . ." Kara sputtered a laugh. "I don't know her *that* well."

"Maybe not. But you seem like the kind of woman who can make anything happen," said Tlaca. "She and I will meet."

The orchestra musicians fell silent as the concertmaster walked to the front of the stage, and the audience settled back in their seats. All except Kara, who leaned forward once more to catch a glimpse of the princess.

She had a charismatic yet commanding presence . . . perfect for a great interview subject *and* ally.

Kara had a feeling they would definitely meet again.

TO BE CONTINUED . . .

ACKNOWLEDGMENTS

Always for my family, friends, fans, and God

For my agent, Jenn, who works her tail off (which is why you can't see it)

For my editor, Pam, who listens to me rant, is incredibly patient, and is always willing to brainstorm

For my executive editor, Maggie, who wears many hats with grace and aplomb

For my freelance editor, Abby, who is annoyingly correct and makes my work stronger

For Orlando, who was there when I started building this Rome

For my publisher, Andrew, who is always as excited about new Supergirl developments as I am

For the New York Public Library, who generously shared their collection of Roman history and culture with me

For the Metropolitan Museum of Art, whose artifact collection is second to none

For Peter David, who created an excellent villain in Gaius Marcus (I tweaked him; hope you don't mind)

For Gary Frank, who put a face to the name

For Jack Kirby, who left behind some wonderful characters

For the creators, writers, cast, and crew of Supergirl, who continue to produce such amazing and inspiring work, including the team at Warner Bros. and the CW, including Greg Berlanti, Robert Rovner, Jessica Queller, Sarah Schechter, Carl Ogawa, Lindsay Kiesel, Janice Aguilar-Herrero, Catherine Shin, Thomas Zellers, Kristin Chin, Josh Anderson and Amy Weingartner.

ABOUT THE AUTHOR

JO WHITTEMORE is the author of numerous fantasy and humor novels for kids, including: The Silverskin Legacy trilogy; *Me & Mom vs. the World*; the Confidentially Yours hexalogy; and *Lights, Music, Code!*, a series novel for Girls Who Code.

Jo is a member of SCBWI (the Society of Children's Book Writers and Illustrators) and is part of the Texas Sweethearts and Scoundrels. She loves to make people laugh; and when she isn't tickling strangers, Jo writes from a secret lair in Austin, Texas, which she shares with her husband.

READ ON FOR A
LOOK AT THE NEXT
ADVENTURE . . .

SUPE

JAMES OLSEN ENVIED SHORT PEOPLE. It was so much easier for them to go undetected in a surveillance van when they slid down in the passenger seat. All he got for his troubles was a backache and leg cramps from pressing his knees against the dashboard. For the phone call he was making, though, it was necessary. If his best friend Winn found out who was on the line, it was all over.

James popped his head up to check on Winn's progress in the FroZone queue, but Winn had stepped away and was shouting into his cell phone, waving his free hand.

"Jimmy?" James's mother spoke in his ear. "I asked you a question."

James slouched in his seat again. "Sorry, Ma, I got distracted. What'd you ask?"

"When are you coming home? It'd be nice if my CEO son could take a break once in a while and visit his mother."

"I know. Sorry," James apologized again. "It's been crazy around here," he said.

And he meant it.

When he'd lived in Metropolis, James had been the *Daily Planet*'s lead photographer and Superman's sidekick. Life had been fairly laid-back. But in National City, between being CatCo's acting CEO and helping Supergirl and the DEO *and* patrolling the city as Guardian at night, James barely had time for himself, let alone other people.

Maybe he noticed it more because he was constantly fighting it, but crime in National City was way higher than in Metropolis. And it was always rising.

The thought was kind of depressing.

"Well, how about I come see you, then?" asked Mrs. Olsen.

"You want to come here?" James repeated, sitting upright. "I don't think that's a good idea, Ma. Have you been watching the news about National City lately?"

"Of course! That Supergirl is amazing. I want to meet her! You know her, right?"

James nodded. "I do, but she's not the only hero in National City. Guardian is making a pretty big name for himself, too."

"Guardian . . . Guardian . . . I don't know him."

"I'm sure you've seen him on the news," James said. "He wears a knight's helmet and body armor with a shield that pops out of his sleeve."

"Oh, that sounds adorable," Mrs. Olsen said.

James rubbed a hand over his shaven head. "No, Ma, Guardian is not adorable."

The passenger door flew open, and James jumped in his seat, looking over at a starry-eyed Winn.

"Are you talking to your mom?" Winn asked, the lower half of his face one huge smile. He stepped onto the sideboard and craned his neck to shout into the mouthpiece of James's phone. "Hi, Mrs. Olsen!"

And just like that, James's one-on-one time with his mom was all over.

Since Winn had been abandoned by *his* mother, and his father was a murderous psychopath, James couldn't deny his best friend the chance to talk with someone parental.

So, with a sigh, he put his mom on speakerphone.

Mrs. Olsen was chuckling. "Hello, Winn, sweetheart. Did you get that sweater I sent?"

"I'm wearing it right now!" Winn grinned and tugged at the front. "It's my official stakeout sweater."

As soon as the words left his mouth, Winn seemed to realize they were the wrong ones.

His grin dropped, James's eyebrows shot up, and the line went quiet.

"Stakeout?" Mrs. Olsen repeated with no less than 100 percent attitude in her voice.

Winn chuckled. "Whaaat?" His voice hit a pitch reserved for opera singers. Winn cleared his throat. "Bad connection. No, I said it's my *takeout* sweater. I wear this all the time when I . . . uh . . . order Chinese food." He flinched and mouthed an apology to James.

"Take me off speaker, son," said Mrs. Olsen.

James's heart skipped a beat, but he did as he was told. Winn sucked in his breath and crept around to the driver's side of the van.

"I know what I heard," Mrs. Olsen informed James. "Now, promise me you two aren't doing anything reckless."

Technically, at that very second, they weren't.

"I promise," James said.

"And promise me you're leaving the crime-fighting to the superheroes."

Guardian was a superhero.

"I promise."

Mrs. Olsen's voice took on its usual loving tone. "All right then. What do you two boys have planned besides Chinese food?"

"Just picking up some ice cream," James said as Winn pulled away from the curb.

James glanced at Winn, whose hands were full of steering wheel and empty of ice cream. James prodded his friend, who arched an eyebrow and nodded at James's phone.

"Uh . . . we're at the front of the line now, Ma," James lied. "I have to let you go."

"All right, honey. But think about what I said about visiting. I miss you!"

"I'll think about it," James promised. "And I miss you, too, Ma. Love you." He ended the call and swiveled in his seat to face Winn. "Dude."

Winn held up a finger. "No, no, no. I do not want to hear it. I just spent twenty minutes in a line *outside*, waiting for ice cream." He looked at James. "Outside. Where the nature is."

"And yet you did not *get* ice cream," James pointed out. "What gives?"

"We have to get back to the DEO. Something big is going down, and they need all hands on deck. Well . . . they need *these* hands on deck." Winn wiggled his fingers.

"Why? What's happening?" James asked.

"Apparently, there's an evil magician on the loose," said Winn.

"Evil magician?" James wrinkled his forehead. "What, like the bad guy from *Harry Potter*?"

Winn tilted his head. "Mm . . . technically, Voldemort is a wizard."

James rolled his eyes. "All right, so what's up with the evil magician?"

"Alex said he's looking for a bell." Winn turned the steering wheel, and the van rounded a corner.

"A bell? I thought magicians were into rabbits," James said. "Why a bell?"

Winn shrugged. "I dunno. They're easier to clean up after? They make more noise when you shake 'em?"

James stared at him. "I really hope you didn't have pets as a kid."

"Relax! I'm kidding," Winn glanced in the side-view mirror as he changed lanes. "Hey, so, you told your mom you were going to think about something. What was it?"

"Oh, she wants to come visit"—James flicked his wrist absentmindedly—"but I told her it's not a good idea. Too dangerous."

Winn snorted and stopped at a red light. "Too dangerous? We have Supergirl to protect us."

James smacked his palm on the armrest of his seat and scowled at Winn.

"Wha . . . in *addition* to Guardian!" Winn amended. "You didn't let me finish."

Static sounded from the back of the van, followed by a woman's voice over the police scanner. "All available units in the area, we've got a robbery in progress at eight-two-five Mandrake. Homeowners say suspect is unarmed but commanding what they believe to be a . . . um . . . dragon."

James and Winn looked at each other.

A chirping sounded over the police scanner, followed by a man's voice. "Unit thirteen here. Can you repeat? It sounded like you said a dragon?"

"Ten-four. Fire and EMS are also en route."

"OK, we can be a few minutes late to the DEO for a *dragon*." Winn pulled to the side of the road and glanced at James. "What do you say, Guardian?"

James unclipped his seat belt. "Time to suit up."

While James got into costume, another call came over the police scanner.

"All units, all units, we've got a robbery in progress at seven-oh-six Mandrake."

"Isn't that across the street from the first break-in?" asked Winn.

"Yeah, it is." Guardian donned his helmet. "Let's see what's going on out there."

He straddled a motorcycle that was latched to the van floor and kicked loose the clasp.

Winn threw open the van doors and pressed a wall-mounted button. "Bombs away," he said as the ramp dropped.

Guardian revved the bike's engine and, with a squeal of tires and cloud of exhaust, took off. He could hear Winn coughing in his comms.

"Thanks for the lung cancer, Showboat," Winn said.

"Anytime." Guardian banked hard right on the corner and shot up Mandrake.

"You're not going to believe this," Winn said over his comms a few minutes later, "but I just heard about *another* robbery on the police scanner. This one at six-five-eight Mandrake. Weird thing is . . . from the looks of the security cameras, the place is empty. Someone made it in and out of there *fast.*"

"A speedster?" asked Guardian.

He, Winn, and Supergirl were all friends with Barry Allen, a speedster code-named Flash from a parallel Earth, so Guardian knew such people existed.

"I don't think so," said Winn. "Just . . . be careful. I'm liking this situation less and less."

"With these robberies one after the other, it sounds

like a crew working their way down the street," Guardian replied. "Find out what's so special about the area."

"Ooh! There's a twenty-four-hour yogurt shop!"

"More special than that, Winn."

Guardian leaned low over the bike and opened the throttle, heading for the dragon-threatened house. No red-and-blue police lights flashed on the street, which meant he was first on the scene. When Guardian dismounted his bike and ran inside, however, he found the owners righting overturned furniture and refilling emptied drawers.

At the sight of Guardian, they gasped, but he raised his hands nonthreateningly.

"I'm here to help. I heard you'd had trouble." He cocked his head to one side. "With a dragon."

A woman in a bathrobe hurried forward. "I know it sounds crazy, but I swear it was here!" she said. "And then suddenly, it vanished."

"A vanishing dragon?" Winn spoke in Guardian's ear. "Sounds like something a *magician* might conjure."

"One that was good at illusions," Guardian agreed out loud.

The woman shook her head. "No, this thing was real! I felt the ground shake when it walked. I felt the heat of its breath."

Guardian watched a teenage boy put his video games back on the shelf. "What did the thief take?" Guardian asked.

"Nothing!" The woman held her arms open. "I mean, I'm relieved, don't get me wrong. We're not rich, but we have—"

"Meredith!" a man shouted at her. "Don't tell masked vigilantes our business!" He gestured to Guardian.

"Nice," Winn said in Guardian's ear. "We're happy to help, grateful citizens."

"Have a good night, folks," Guardian told them, ignoring Winn. "And stay safe."

Guardian trotted down the stairs. "I'm headed for seven-oh-six now. Hopefully we'll find something more promising there."

"Don't bother," said Winn over the clacking of keys. "The owner responded to his security company and said nothing was taken."

"On to the next one then." Guardian pulled his motorcycle up to 658 Mandrake, which turned out to be a pottery store. As he stepped through the shattered doorframe, his boots crunched on glass *and* porcelain. While the glass debris diminished the farther he got from the entrance, the porcelain pieces increased in volume. He scanned the store's shelves, all of which were now empty, their contents smashed on the floor and slowly being ground under Guardian's boots.

"Eesh. No wonder Pottery Barn switched to selling furniture," Winn said in Guardian's ear.

"Someone deliberately broke these," said Guardian.

"How much do you want to bet it was our missing magician, looking for the bell?"

"You might be right," Guardian replied, approaching the manager's office. "I . . . what was that?"

A low rumbling down one of the aisles drew his attention. Guardian turned and followed the sound.

"Winn, who or what is in here with me?" Guardian whispered.

"What are you talking about?" asked Winn. "I told you that the place is empty—WHOA! James, get out of there now!"

"What? Why?" Guardian backed up, deploying his shield. "What is it?"

"Something you're *very* ill-equipped to face without a fire extinguisher." The panic was rising in Winn's voice. "You found the dragon!"

Suddenly, the interior of the pottery store was alight with orange flames.

Guardian crouched and raised his shield, feeling the heat all the way through his suit. As the fire died, he saw its source: a green, lizard-like creature that filled the space from floor to ten-foot ceiling with its presence.

The dragon screeched and took a floor-shaking step toward Guardian.

"That's my cue to leave," he said, sprinting toward the storefront.

"Wait a minute, wait a minute. You can't!" said Winn. "There's someone trapped in the store office."

Guardian skidded to a halt. "What?"

"I just saw movement in the office."

Guardian growled and whirled around. "You and I need to talk about what the word 'empty' means."

"It's pitch-black inside!" Winn said defensively. "I didn't notice until they lit up their phone."

After a few calming breaths, Guardian doubled back. He chanced a glimpse at the dragon, but it had thankfully stomped away to explore another aisle.

Guardian pressed his face close to the office door. "Is someone there?" he asked as loudly as he dared.

"Yes! Help!" A woman's muffled voice carried through from inside, and the door handle jiggled. "He locked me in here!"

"Guardian, watch your back!" Winn shouted in his ear.

Guardian turned as the dragon lashed its tail, leaping just before the tail connected.

Unfortunately, he didn't predict the tail making a return trip.

Guardian's feet were swept out from under him and he flopped onto his back.

"James!" Winn shouted.

"I'm good," he said, coughing.

But when Guardian sat up, he realized that wasn't quite true.

The dragon, feeling its tail strike something, had circled back around. It was now advancing on Guardian and slowly widening its jaws.

"Your armor is only heatproof to five hundred Fahrenheit," Winn warned as Guardian got to his feet. "If that thing gets any closer . . ."

"I won't let it." Guardian thrust out his right arm and clenched his fist. A grappling hook shot from his wrist-mounted holster and wrapped around a display rack next to the dragon.

Digging his heels into the floor, Guardian jerked on the grappling hook's line. With a creak, the rack tipped over, falling on the dragon . . . and then falling through it. The dragon continued to stand there with a display rack through its torso.

"Wait. What?" asked Winn.

James removed his helmet and stared in awe. "It's not real." He approached the dragon, ignoring the tinny sound of Winn yelling from inside the helmet.

The dragon spewed a stream of fire, but this time, James felt nothing. Then, without so much as a screech, the dragon disappeared.

James put his helmet back on. "Winn, the dragon isn't real. The heat, the fire . . . none of it."

"You couldn't have figured that out with your helmet *on*?" Winn's voice sounded almost hysterical.

A pounding came from the office door, and Guardian trotted over.

"Almost forgot." In a louder voice, he said, "Stand clear!"

He lifted his right leg and kicked out hard, knocking the door loose from its hinges.

Guardian stepped into the office, where a woman cowered in the corner.

"Is it over?" she asked in a quavering voice.

Guardian nodded. "You're safe now." He offered her a hand up. "Any idea what the person who did this was looking for?"

The woman wrapped her arms around herself. "Uh . . . yeah." She sniffled and wiped at her face. "He mentioned something about a bell. A special bell."

"That's our magician, all right." Winn's voice was in Guardian's ear again. "Also, I've been analyzing the area. The people here call it Little Bohemia, and it appears to be the nose ring capital of the world. It's also a hot spot for magic practitioners."

Guardian turned away from the woman and trotted toward the exit. "If that's the case, I'm guessing this won't be the magician's last stop of the night," he told Winn.

"I'll contact NCPD," Winn said. "And then we really need to get to the DEO."

"I'm on my way to the van," Guardian said, hopping onto the bike and shaking his head.

Real dragon or no, his mom *definitely* wasn't coming to National City anytime soon.